Cover Copy

He will sacrifice anything to protect her.

It's been a year since Saria Sands entered The Program, her last chance to stay one step ahead of a relentless killer. When Bodyguard and Weapons expert Ben Hammers sends her on a private yacht to the South Pacific, Saria agrees. But confined in close quarters together on the yacht, Saria can't help desiring more with her mysterious protector.

Ben Hammers will do anything to protect Saria. She's more than just a job. Protecting the innocent is Ben's only way to right a wrong he's kept hidden his whole life, a secret that has kept him from forming a connection with any woman, let alone the one he wants more than anything.

Ben knows he can't let his guard down. But the more time he spends with Saria, the further he finds himself slipping...

Books by Joanne Wadsworth

The Matheson Brothers Series
Highlander's Desire, Book One
Highlander's Passion, Book Two
Highlander's Seduction, Book Three
Highlander's Kiss, Book Four
Highlander's Heart, Book Five
Highlander's Sword, Book Six
Highlander's Bride, Book Seven
Highlander's Caress, Book Eight
Highlander's Touch, Book Nine
Highlander's Shifter, Book Ten
Highlander's Claim, Book Eleven
Highlander's Courage, Book Twelve
Highlander's Mermaid, Book Thirteen

Highlander Heat Series
Highlander's Castle, Book One
Highlander's Magic, Book Two
Highlander's Charm, Book Three
Highlander's Guardian, Book Four
Highlander's Faerie, Book Five
Highlander's Champion, Book Six
Highlander's Captive (Short Story)

Billionaire Bodyguards Series
Billionaire Bodyguard Attraction, Book One
Billionaire Bodyguard Boss, Book Two
Billionaire Bodyguard Fling, Book Three

Books by Joanne Wadsworth

Regency Brides Series

The Duke's Bride, Book One
The Earl's Bride, Book Two
The Wartime Bride, Book Three
The Earl's Secret Bride, Book Four
The Prince's Bride, Book Five
Her Pirate Prince, Book Six

Princesses of Myth Series

Protector, Book One
Warrior, Book Two
Hunter (Short Story - Included in Warrior, Book Two)
Enchanter, Book Three
Healer, Book Four
Chaser, Book Five

BILLIONAIRE BODYGUARD
Boss

Billionaire Bodyguards, Book Two

JOANNE WADSWORTH

Billionaire Bodyguard Boss
ISBN-13: 978-1-99-003429-9
Copyright © 2015, Joanne Wadsworth
Cover Art by Joanne Wadsworth
First electronic publication: August 2015

Joanne Wadsworth
http://www.joannewadsworth.com

AUTHOR'S NOTE:
This book is a work of fiction. The names, characters, places, and incidents are products of the writer's imagination or have been used fictitiously and are not to be construed as real. Any resemblance to persons, living or dead, actual events, locale or organizations is entirely coincidental. The author does not have any control over and does not assume any responsibility for third-party websites or their content.

Published in the United States of America

First digital publication: August 2015
First print publication: August 2015

Dedication

This one's for all those authors who opened up a world of adventure and inspired me to write the same.

Acknowledgements

Huge thanks go to my hubby, Jason, and kiddies, Marisa, Caleb, Cruise and Rocco, an incredibly supportive family who allow me so much time to write. My love for you is endless.

I also have the most amazing editor, Penny Barber. The absolute best.

For my readers, I can't thank you enough for joining me, and taking this journey to where imagination and magic.

Chapter 1

"How can you laze about and not want to get up and move?" Saria Sands paced the glorious top poolside deck of Tyler Whitehall's luxury super-yacht as it cruised the warm waters of the South Pacific toward Fiji. Her identical twin lay sprawled on a lounger before her, so cool and calm, while her anxiety level kept rising.

"This is called a holiday. The whole point of one is to embrace the peace and solitude." Lydia propped her aviator sunglasses up with one finger and eyed her from underneath the dark rims. "The baddies got locked away and there's no longer a killer chasing us. You need to sit, kick back, and relax."

"I keep looking over my shoulder, expecting Ben to be right there. Don't you miss him?" She and Lydia had spent the past year in a safe house with a full time bodyguard, and Ben Hammers had guarded them with his life. Comfort and security only came when he stood at her back.

"No, Saria, but then you depended on him far more than I ever did. I've also had Tyler guarding me these past two months while you and I've been apart, and yes, I'd miss him like crazy if he weren't here. Or in my bed." Smiling, she cast a glance at Tyler and his brother as they swam lengths.

"I can't believe you're getting married, or that you're pregnant." That had been the last thing Saria had expected to hear when she'd finally reconnected with her sister two days ago.

"Neither can I, but both events are nice surprises." Lydia frowned as she eyed her. "Look at you. You need to chill, and the only way that's going to happen is if you give Ben a call. He'd understand if you did, and the sat phone's just across the way in the captain's control room."

"I'm tempted." Beyond tempted. She itched to run across the deck, grab that phone and jab in his number.

"I wouldn't be surprised if he felt as lost as you." Lydia tucked her white cotton swimsuit cover-up under her bare legs and wriggled her toes.

"Ha. That's doubtful. He's always been a complete professional. Feeling lost isn't even an emotion on his radar."

"I'm not sure. I've seen the way he looks at you." Lydia tapped her chin.

"He looks at me because watching one's client comes with the job." Still, temptation ground at her. She nudged her sister's stretched legs and Lydia wriggled over. She sat next to her and arched a brow. "Okay, exactly how does he look at me? And be specific." A loaded question, but she needed an answer.

"As if he's both fascinated and frustrated." Grinning, Lydia sat straighter. "At times I'd see him standing behind you, his hands lifted and his fingers a whisper away. He'd inch closer as if he wanted to touch you, then when he realized what he was doing, he'd grimace and back away."

"Are you certain? I never saw any such thing. He touched me only if necessary."

"I'm positive. And let's not forget he started sleeping with you while I was away, which goes way beyond touching in my book."

"He slept with me for a very good reason, to allay my fears when you went through re-identification. And still, he didn't touch me, unless you count the odd pat on the back when I was sobbing my heart out." Which couldn't have been more vexing. How she'd wanted him to hold her, to embrace his strength and siphon some for herself. Yes, he was her bodyguard, but also her friend. Friends hugged from time to time. Even now fear gripped her in its icy hands, no matter she was safe and amongst family she trusted.

"Take a deep breath and see if that helps you relax. Nice and slow." Lydia squeezed her hand, concern radiating in her gaze.

"What will help is seeing the bodyguard I don't need any more now our case is almost closed up." She fidgeted with an unraveled string dangling from her shirt's cotton hem, wound it around her finger then tugged it off. It snapped in the right spot but then loosened another inch. Stupid cotton. Huh, even it matched her unraveled thoughts. During her time in the safe house, Ben had erected a professional wall between them and she hadn't had a hope of tearing it down, not when doing so would have meant him being pulled from her job. Something she'd never allow when she'd needed him just as much as she'd needed Lydia.

As she relaxed her cheek against Lydia's shoulder, her sister's sweet vanilla scent surrounded and comforted her. "At twenty-one, I should've been able to handle a little separation from you, but it wasn't possible. Your life was on the line, and the danger you were in was all I could think about."

"Those were the hardest weeks for me too." Lydia wrapped an arm around her shoulders and sniffed. "There were nights where I'd lie outside in the dark and stare at the sky wondering if you were looking at the same stars as me. Re-identification was incredibly painful, and I hated you'd soon have to suffer the same loneliness as me."

"I felt lonely anyway, re-identification or not. The pain went both ways." Their twin bond was strong and always had been, no matter any distance separating them. She pulled a lock of Lydia's glossy brown hair, now dyed back from the bright red her handler, Agent Gilchrist, had disguised her with. "I missed you, badly. Losing you was like losing a part of me."

"I missed you too, and I'm glad you're here with me now rather than still at the safe house. I wish our family were as well." A tear slid down Lydia's cheek and Saria wiped it away with her thumb.

"Don't cry, or you'll make me start. Ben said its best they remain at home until all the loose ends in our case are tidied away. We'll all be back together again soon." It wasn't fair her sister had to get married without their parents and brothers here, but their continued safety had to be maintained.

"What do you think of Tyler's family? At least they get to be here."

"I love how they watch out for you. They're so attentive." Tyler and his three brothers owned Whitehall Shipping, and this super-yacht formed part of that fleet. Unfortunately, they were here though, because they'd gotten caught up in hers and Lydia's case only a few short weeks—

"Excuse me, ladies." Henry, one of the wait staff, stood over her in his crisp crew whites holding a silver tray with drinks.

She patted her thumping heartbeat. "You shouldn't sneak up on a girl like that."

"My apologies, Miss Saria. I didn't mean to frighten you."

"No, it's not you. My nerves are shot." As they had been for months now.

"Perhaps I might whistle then the next time I approach. Master Tyler did warn me to take extra care." Henry had worked for the Whitehalls for years, and when Ben had handed her over into Tyler's care, he'd made sure all on board were aware of her fears.

How she hated those fears. She should have been able to break the excessive worrying now she and Lydia were back together again, but it appeared it would take more than two days to override the year of complete agitation running from a killer had caused her. "Whistling would be perfect. Thank you, Henry."

"Then that's what I'll do. I have your drink." Henry passed her a lemon and lime bitters, and her sister a glass of iced tea before stepping across to the wooden slatted side table and setting the men's drinks down on black leather placemats for when they finished swimming in the pool. He arranged a bowl of nuts and snacks on the table center then whistled a jaunty tune as he strolled to the stairwell.

"I think you should ring Ben." Lydia playfully dunked her ice with the bright red straw then sipped her drink. "It'd give you some peace of mind, and it's clear you need to hear his voice."

"It'd be more relaxed if I had him here. Surely bodyguards need to unwind too. He should have come."

"See, you do like him."

"He's also thousands of miles away in Auckland."

"Then I'll call him for you." Lydia yawned and patted her mouth. Her eyelids fluttered and she shoved them back open.

"Are you getting enough sleep? It is your first trimester and you need to rest."

"It's not so much the baby but Tyler who enjoys keeping me awake at night. Which I quite like by the way." She set her drink down and smiling, curled onto her side and slid her hand under her cheek. "I might just have a nap though while he's busy burning off some energy."

"Then I'll leave you to your rest." If only Saria could sleep herself. Her worry over the killer, even though he'd been caught, still kept her awake no matter the hour of the day or night. She rose, straightened her yellow tank top over her blue cutoffs and wandered to the top deck's waist-high glass railing. Four floors below, the waves sloshed against the side of the ship.

Ben would love the solitude here, along with the miles upon

miles of endless ocean. Not one possible killer gunning for her in sight. She lifted her face to the heavens and let out a heartfelt sigh. The sun shone high, the sky a soft blue with only a wisp of cloud on the horizon. The ocean breezed played over her skin and lifted her brown hair with a gentle flutter at her back.

"Are you okay, Saria? You looked anxious before when Henry arrived." Dripping water, Luke, Tyler's youngest brother, eased in beside her in his blue swim trunks. He shook his dark head and sent drops flying. "The lovebirds are finally chilling. You should too."

"I would if I weren't so worried about Ben. It's not easy being separated from someone when you've come to rely on them so solidly."

"The best thing to do is focus on someone or something else for a change." Luke draped a wet arm around her shoulders. "How about a game of cards? You can focus on trying to beat me."

"The only card game I know is snap. Not much focus needed there."

"Then I'll teach you how to play poker. Mum and Gabriella loved the game. We often play it in memory of them." Two years ago, his mother and sister-in-law had passed away in a terrible car accident. That had left Tyler's eldest brother raising his young son alone. The Whitehall family had experienced so much loss of late.

"I'd like that. Although, I have to warn you, Ben tried to teach me how to play. He failed miserably, or I did in learning, however you want to look at it." It hadn't helped Ben had always sat so close when he'd been teaching her. Her focus had veered toward him and not the game. Her bodyguard had deep blue eyes she wanted to drown in and a presence of strength that engrossed her.

"We'll find Dylan, and he can join us. He's a great teacher." Luke smiled with big dimples. "He also thinks he's the best at poker, and I love taking him down."

"I'm all for some sibling rivalry." She rolled her shoulders and tried to relax. Lydia was lucky to have such a wonderful new family.

Although they were now hers too.

What her twin gained, so did she.

"Show me the way, Luke. It's time to unwind."

* * * *

Ben shoved his black shirtsleeves to his elbows as he strode into the safe house bedroom he'd shared with Saria for the past two months. The cleaners had stripped the queen-sized bed and the last of her belongings, now boxed, sat on the plush gray-carpeted floor next to his gear.

Saria's little touches around the room, from the vase of white lilies that graced the nightstand to her favorite vanilla and strawberry scented candles, had infused this space with such sweet elegance. Now, all gone, tossed out with the rubbish or packed away. Her nursing journals no longer lay scattered across the corner desk she'd called her own for the past year.

After shutting the security-latched window the cleaner had left open, he drew the lacy net curtains across, then slid her box on top of his and carried it down the hallway. At the front door with its crooked brass number ten, the ghostlike scent of home baking tickled his nose. If Saria hadn't been studying for her nursing finals, she'd had her nose buried in a recipe book. Every day she'd cooked, from cakes and cookies to the meals they'd eaten. Caring for others relaxed her, had taken her mind off her fears. None of his foster parents ever cared for him the way she had. Hell, he missed her—a totally unacceptable emotion in his job.

Down the stone path he trudged, then popped the trunk of his Jaguar and arranged their boxes inside. He lugged his cell phone from his pocket and skimmed the buttons. The ship's sat phone number, emblazoned in his mind as well as programmed into his speed dial, taunted him. Saria had left two days ago, and his fingers twitched to call her. Hearing her sweet voice would ease some of his concerns. Had her fears subsided now she had Lydia back? He hoped so. He longed to see her stand strong and take back the courage and strength she'd lost during the time Lydia had gone through re-identification.

Unable to hold off any longer, he pressed the speed dial number then rapped one foot on the concrete driveway within the quiet Auckland city suburb.

"Tyler Whitehall."

"It's Ben." He stopped rapping as one of his best mate's voices flowed down the line.

"Hey, I just hung up from Brigs and was about to call you. Sorry about the short notice, but Lydia and I are getting hitched in Fiji, and I need you and Brigs there. Do you feel up to a trip to Resort Island?"

He'd never seen a man more dedicated to the woman he loved. Tyler had even taken bullets for Lydia and nearly died. He'd always have his respect and admiration. "Absolutely. How long do I have to get there?"

The girls' case, almost tidied away, made his answer an easy one.

"It only takes three days to organize a license with the Fijian authorities, so the ceremony will be at the end of the week. Brigs has already booked his seat and is holding one for you on the same flight. He sorted it all out online while we chatted. The plane leaves at midnight and arrives at Nadi at three tomorrow morning."

"Sounds good to me. I'll call and confirm the seat." Now he'd have the chance to see Saria in person, to make certain she was well. A touch of the tight pressure in his chest eased. He missed her, and as a bodyguard shouldn't miss his client. He'd have to get his wayward emotions under control before he arrived.

"Great. I went ahead and ordered the chopper for you both. The pilot is leaving Nadi's airbase at five AM, which means you won't get any sleep, but at least you'll be here by dawn, around the same time we're due to sail in. I'll have a cabin made ready for you both. Hey, how's the girls' case going?"

"Agent Gilchrist is still tidying away the details, though I've done all I can. I actually rang to check in on Saria. How's she doing?"

"Still quite jumpy. We're all trying to work on unwinding her which is not an easy task." Tyler's clomping footsteps echoed down the line then a door banged shut. "I'm taking the phone to Saria now. Luke took her downstairs to play cards in the hope of distracting her. Luke mentioned she's worried about you too."

"She shouldn't be. I'm not in any danger." When her fears had first arisen and she hadn't been getting any sleep, he'd taken her to see a therapist. The woman had assured him everything would blow over once Saria became more settled. The therapist had instructed him to give Saria whatever comfort she needed, and if that meant remaining close to her at night when she suffered the most, then to do so in a non-threatening way. He'd delivered, or at least he'd tried without stepping over that frustrating bodyguard-client line.

"Ben, living together for a year, no matter the circumstances, brings people closer together. Whether there's danger or not, she's going to worry. You should've rung her and touched base by now. Girls need that," Tyler advised.

"Living together, yes, but I kept a professional distance even when I slept beside her."

"And therein lies your problem. You allowed Saria to become dependent on you, and far more than I've ever seen you allow with another client before."

"Her physical and emotional welfare were my responsibility, and I did whatever it took to ease her fears. She's more than a client. She's a friend. Put her on. Let me speak to her." He couldn't have her suffering. His gut would be in turmoil and eat him up.

"Almost there. I was poolside, and she's two flights down. Saria, the phone's for you."

"Is it Ben?" Saria's voice rolled over him, soothing him. "Ben, is everything okay? Are you all right?"

"I'm fine, Saria. How are you feeling?"

"I'll feel better if you keep talking. I need to hear your voice."

"I'm outside the house now and have the last of your things in the boot of my car. What do you want me to do with them?"

"Just keep a hold of what's there for me until I can grab it off you. Did you hear Tyler and Lydia are getting married? He asked her the day we set sail." An edge of expectation laced her tone and he sensed her next question before she asked it. "Lydia said Tyler wanted you and Brigs to come for the wedding."

At least he could allay that fear.

"We are." He propped his butt on the hood of his car and stroked the shiny silver paintwork. "Brigs and I are flying out tonight. We'll be there by dawn tomorrow."

"Then you have to ring me, before you takeoff and again when you land. Sorry, stupid fears, but you have to."

"It's no problem." He'd do whatever it took to ensure she remained at ease. "I'd have called before now if I'd known what you were going through. You want to talk about it?"

"I'm still not sleeping well at night. It's difficult when you're not beside me."

"You've got your sister."

"I miss you too."

"You're not permitted to miss your bodyguard."

"I knew you'd say that." She clicked her tongue as if telling him off. "Will your office run smoothly with you gone?"

"My office assistant is beyond organized." His specialist

team of bodyguards worked all over the country and Gladys ensured everything ticked along. He accepted jobs from government officials right through to local law enforcement. Long or short term. He never turned anything of value down.

"Saria, get back here now. Dylan's cheating and I need your help." The deep male voice rang in Ben's ears.

"Is that Luke?" he asked, clenching his fist.

"Yes, and we're playing poker. I'm finally getting a good grasp on the game."

"How's that?" He'd tried to teach her, but gotten nowhere.

"Well, I have to remove a piece of clothing every time I get an ace in the hand."

"What?" He jolted upright. "Are you telling me you're playing strip poker?" Damn Luke. He'd told Tyler's brothers they had to watch out for her, not take advantage of her. "I'll kill him."

"Calm down. I get to put that clothing back on if I win that hand. Luke insists it's to help me concentrate on the good card I just got dealt. It's a little bit of reverse psychology, and it's working. I'm incredibly focused on not ending up naked."

"You have to watch Luke." Luke was the youngest, and at twenty-three, a terrible flirt. His short nails bit into his palm. No one was permitted to see Saria naked, not even him. One morning he'd actually caught her coming out of her bathroom after she'd showered. She'd been wrapped in a fleecy white towel that barely covered her breasts and bottom. That image would be forever seared into his mind. He'd certainly struggled to turn around and walk back out again when all he'd wanted to do was strip her bare, toss her onto the bed and touch her as he'd always longed to. He groaned then forced his wayward thoughts back into the dark hole they needed to remain in. "No nakedness is permitted on board that ship. You hear me?"

"Is that an order, Hammers?" One sexy smooth tone, the words delivered in a way that had those thoughts slipping free again. Hell, he loved it when she called him Hammers.

"If you ever wish to play strip poker, then let me teach you." Damn. He had to get himself under control. He'd taken an oath to protect her, which meant even from himself.

"Is that a promise?" Was she flirting back with him?

"No."

"Spoilsport." A soft sigh.

"Morning there, neighbor." The elderly man from across the other side of the road waved as he strolled along the pavement.

"Morning," he called back and turned away so he wouldn't invoke further conversation. "Saria, I need to go. I'm attracting some attention when I shouldn't be."

"Where are you?"

"In the driveway, but wishing I was throttling Luke instead. You're not to remove any more clothing, okay?" Two birds shrieked from the highest branch of the old oak tree gracing the front lawn as if adding their agreement.

"Funny, but sure. I'll let Luke know he'll have to tangle with you if I do. Don't forget to call me tonight. I'll be waiting."

"I'll call you when I get to the airport, about ten. Talk to you soon." He hated hanging up, but he did before he gave in and stayed on the line with her. He'd have to find a way to insert some distance between them while at the island, but at the right time so they both managed to come out of this codependency they'd formed unscathed. He'd certainly never experienced these kinds of emotions with any other client he'd lived with, but then Saria was different. He'd known from the moment he'd met her that maintaining any emotional distance wouldn't be easy. She loved with all her heart, and made his heart want far more than he could ever have.

The secret of his unfortunate birth had decreed his future. One of utter solitude.

Which meant Saria was out of bounds.

His disgusting father had so much to answer for.

* * * *

In bed, Saria tossed and turned, the white sheet covering her more like a stifling weight than a piece of thin cotton. The bedside clock ticked over to 6.00 AM. Ben should have called eight incessantly long hours ago, yet every time she picked up the sat phone and tried to get a dial tone, nothing happened. Last night the captain had said they'd moved out of satellite range. They needed to move back within it, or even better, arrive at the island, which had its own cell phone tower and connection to the mainland. She had to know if Ben had traveled safely.

She untangled her legs from the sheet, shoved her feet over the side of the queen-sized bed and palms on the windowsill, leaned her forehead against the wide sheet of darkened glass. Along the horizon, red blazed across the dawn sky and the ship slowed as the tropical island appeared like a hidden treasure within the expanse of blue. A long wharf jutted out, and at the top end of the walkway, a dark-skinned Polynesian man with springy black hair waved them in toward their berth.

The motor rumbled as the captain reversed into their slot, and the islander in his yellow shorts and polo with the resort's logo emblazoned on it, snatched the end of a coiled mooring rope and tossed it to a crewmember waiting at the stern. The rope tightened and the ship knocked gently against the piling and settled.

Past the wharf, a clear white sand beach curved around the bay, and a mass of swaying palm and coconut trees gave glimpses through the foliage of the resort beyond.

Overhead, the whop-whop of blades drummed a soulful tune. Ben was choppering in at dawn. Her heart pounded as the white and blue aircraft flew in and landed with a soft bump on the concrete helipad beside the wire-fenced tennis courts.

The blades came to a whirring stop and two men jumped down then slung large brown army duffels over their shoulders.

The first man jogged toward the wharf, his face hidden in shadow as he held a black cap in place. He hauled something from his pocket, jabbed at it then pressed it to his ear while the second man caught him up. The man who followed was impossible to misplace with his bronze Samoan skin and black curly hair cropped close to his head. Brigs. He wore long charcoal colored chinos and a black and white checked shirt, his favorite colors.

The sat phone trilled and she grabbed it off the bedside table. "That better be you, Ben Hammers."

"I'm coming. About to board now." He bounded from the wharf into the rear of the ship, his cap sailing free and smacking into Brigs's chest as he jogged up the gangplank behind him. "Neither Brigs or I have been able to get through to you since we left Auckland. The satellite was down. Which floor are you on?"

"Ground floor, first door on your left when you hit the passage—"

Her door banged open and Ben strode in. He hung up, tossed his cell phone on the dresser and shut the door behind him. He was finally here. His windblown blond hair brushed his shoulders, the longer length always making her yearn to run her fingers through it. "I'm sorry I couldn't call. You haven't been too worried, have you?"

"I'd like to say no." She just wanted to haul him to her and hug him, not that he'd ever allow such a touch. Sleep deprived, she wobbled as she set the phone down.

"You knew I'd be here at dawn." He shoved a hand through his hair, tossing those gorgeous locks around.

"That didn't stop me from worrying."

"Did you sleep at all?" He dropped his bag on the white leather couch along the wall, edged around the bed then brushed in behind her. "I don't like those dark circles under your eyes. Lean back against me."

"Are you sure? That would require us touching."

"That's an order, Miss Sands. Lean back."

"Thank you." She slowly relaxed against him. His solid presence, an instant balm to her senses, soothed her as nothing else could. She tipped her head back until it rested on his shoulder, and every tortuous second of the past few days she'd been without him slowly dissolved.

"Is that better?" He stroked her hip and she jumped at the touch then quickly jammed her hand over his.

"Yes, although I really must look like a mess for you to allow this kind of touch."

"I'm not your bodyguard anymore, and those strict rules are gone. A little touch is allowed. Now, get into bed. You clearly need some sleep."

"But you just got here." She didn't care to move, not when she'd lose this precious moment. She twined her fingers through his, and more of his warmth settled over her.

"I'll stay for a bit." He leaned forward, bending her at the waist as he lifted her tangled sheet. "Please. I don't like seeing you this exhausted. You're supposed to be on vacation." Soft words, a whisper in her ear.

"That's what Lydia said." She crawled in and patted the space beside her. "Hop in. There's loads of room for two."

He pursed his lips then nodded. "I guess one more night in your bed won't hurt." He shut the pale blue blinds, toed off his black boots and tucked them beside the built-in caramel-painted drawers. As he unbuckled his belt, his gaze moved around the room. "That's a nice fish tank. I wouldn't have thought to bring the marine life inside."

"Tyler's mother decorated this yacht before she passed. I love it." The cylinder tank, standing floor to ceiling in the corner, held an envious number of exotic fish. They darted in and around the pretty, underwater stone castle, rocks, and swishing reeds. Oxygen bubbles floated to the surface and popped along the top.

"Mrs. Whitehall was an amazing woman. So was

Gabriella." He slid open his black shirt's top two opal buttons, hauled the snug cotton over his head and draped the shirt on top of the dresser.

His broad shoulders and heavily muscled chest had her mouth watering and fingertips tingling. She wanted to trace each ridged ab and defined pec and not stop.

"I've forgotten how hot the tropics are, and the day's barely begun." He slumped onto the bed in his black jeans.

"Take your pants off then." Yeah, a needy request, but she didn't care. "I promise not to pounce if I see more skin than usual."

"I wouldn't let you pounce anyway." A twinkle lit his beautiful sky-blue eyes.

"And I'm curious to learn if you wear boxers or briefs." She rolled onto her side, wrinkling her buttery colored sleep-shorts higher. With one elbow wedged up, she propped her head into her upturned palm. "Indulge me, Hammers."

"Indulging would be dangerous. But it is hot."

"Take them off. I know you could easily hold off little-old-me."

"Sure, but close your eyes."

"Not a chance."

He chuckled, released the button on his jeans and slid his zipper down.

She held her breath.

He shoved the denim down his powerful thighs and kicked his jeans away. Smooth black silk boxers, sitting incredibly low on his hips, gave a tease of blond hair narrowing down his rigid belly and disappearing within. Her breath whooshed out and he eyed her. "Are you all right?"

"Yes, all we need now are some cards and I'll be set for an actual game of strip poker. I'm certain you'd lose."

"Or maybe you would." He fixed the thin strap of her singlet top that had slid off her shoulder. "What are you thinking right now?"

"I'm wondering how quickly you could disarm me if I attempted to make a move."

"Less than a second." He draped the bed sheet over his lower body, and she lost half her glorious sight. "Which means you're not permitted to. I don't want to hurt you, and I am trained to immobilize any threat."

"And you consider me a threat?"

"Of the greatest sort. I don't do relationships, Saria. I've told you that before."

Yes, he'd told her that the night he'd started sleeping in her bed. He'd made his position more than clear, that their new arrangement was necessary because of what her therapist had said. "I've never asked for a relationship, and being stuck in The Program made that impossible. Some fun though would be nice." Slowly, she stretched her fingers and hovered her hand over his chest. She waited for him to halt her, but the seconds ticked by. "You're not stopping me."

"You haven't done anything yet."

"I said I'm after some fun." She pressed down and with lightning speed, he trapped her fingers against his warm skin. His heart beat soundly under her palm.

"Fun isn't permitted between us." He rolled toward her, his brows slashing down. "Clients have the potential to form an attachment to their bodyguard, and at times bodyguards can become as dependent, needing to keep an overly watchful eye and all."

"I might be dependent on you, but I like it."

"We'll muddle through and find a way to break our codependency."

"Muddling is good, breaking is not." She leaned in, rubbed her nose against his. "You should know I've fantasized about kissing you."

"Breaking our bonds means no kissing."

"I've also fantasized about you kissing me."

"You're not being very helpful, Saria. You promised not to pounce, which you are."

"And you said you wouldn't let me. I also noticed your last answer wasn't a direct no."

"Taking my pants off gave you the wrong idea." He pressed forward with his body and steered her back onto her side before rolling back to his. "I want you to sleep. You need the rest and so do I. Tomorrow I'll get my own room and we'll begin on inserting some space. A little at a time so our codependency has a chance of retracting."

"Sleep and retracting are technical terms that just went right over my head. Sorry, but you're out of luck." She wriggled one leg over his. "I want to feel your mouth on mine, to see how deep this connection between us goes."

"There's no connection." He stroked her upper leg. Sure there wasn't.

"Kiss me, or else I'll kiss you."

"Did you just dare me?"

"I did. What are you going to do about it, Hammers?"

"Show you I'm right." He kissed her then jerked away. "See."

"I saw nothing." She touched her lips to his, whisper soft. "I haven't told you this before, but I have two fears, losing you and Lydia. I trust you, like I trust no other. Having some fun won't hurt. I'm not asking for a relationship."

"I have issues."

Which had to be about his family. He never spoke of them, but she'd once probed Brigs who'd been with Ben since their army days, and he'd told her Ben had grown up moving from one foster home to another.

"There are bad genes in my stock, and I have no intention of spreading any of it." He dipped his head to her neck and nuzzled her ear. "I missed your scent, like vanilla and strawberries. Maybe you can loan me one of your candles.”

"Wouldn't you rather have a loan of me?”

"Nope, bad genes, remember?”

"I'm protected, not that you have bad genes.”

He pulled back and looked into her eyes. "I'm inexperienced, Saria. I never intended to have sex, ever.”

"What? You're thirty-two.” He must be kidding.

"Which goes to prove how very insistent I've been.”

"I'm a virgin too.” The words popped out. "I mean, running from a killer and completing my nursing degree put a squash on finding a guy.” She swirled a finger over his chest. "I have a proposition for you, one you need to listen to.” One she intended to get a yes for.

Chapter 2

"I don't do propositions either." Ben could've kicked himself for allowing himself to touch Saria. What the hell had he been thinking to give in and kiss her, even that peck?

"At least hear me—"

"Saria. You in there?" Lydia's voice rang out from the other side of the door.

He couldn't have been more grateful for the interruption.

"I'm here."

"Brigs said Ben was with you. You okay?"

"He is." She tapped his nose. "Don't look so relieved. I'll be back to speak of that proposition the moment I get rid of my sister." Saria crawled over his feet then scrambled to the door and opened it. With one sexy hip resting against the doorjamb and a peek of creamy skin showing between her sleep top and waistband, she smiled at her sister. "Hey, Ben's sleeping in here for the night, I mean day. I didn't manage to get any sleep last night, and he didn't get much either."

"I'm sorry. You should have said." Lydia squeezed her sister's shoulder. "You look a bit flushed."

Those long luscious legs of hers were barely covered with fabric. Those cotton shorts were far too short.

"Ben and I were having a heated discussion."

One Ben had no intention of Lydia hearing the finer details

about. Propped on his elbows, he strove to change the subject. "Congrats on the upcoming wedding, Lydia."

"Thanks. Tyler and I are actually catching the chopper out to the mainland so we can organize our marriage license. We have to head to the courthouse, and he doesn't want to wait."

"How long will you be gone?" Saria grasped Lydia's hand.

"Half a day, maybe more if we take in some sightseeing." Lydia eyed him. "Can you watch Saria for me since I'm leaving?"

"Of course. You don't even need to ask. Where's Brigs?"

"He's in the cabin at the end of the passageway, last door on your right. No one's allowed to disturb him though. His orders since he wanted to catch up on some lost sleep too." Lydia arched a brow at her sister. "You're not allowed to worry too much, and I'll call you the second we reach Nadi."

"Make sure you do." Saria dragged her into a tight hug. "Travel safely."

"We will." Lydia rubbed Saria's back, then waved at him.

Saria shut the door with a gentle click, leaned her forehead against the thick wood and sniffed. Her shoulders shook.

"No crying." He jumped up, scooped her into his arms and carried her back. "Lydia will be fine. It's a short flight. No big deal."

"I'm sorry. She and I have been back together for such a short time." Tears coursed down her cheeks. "I can't stand this stupid weakness."

"Your phobia isn't a weakness. It's a pain in the ass, but you'll get through it." He tucked her under the sheet and curled around her. "You're one of the strongest people I know."

"You always say that, but I don't feel it." She stared at him, the lost brown depths of her eyes dragging him in. "I'm going to take this opportunity while you're here though to beat this fear into submission. With both you and Lydia close, there's no reason why I can't."

"Good, then to do so, you need some rest. I'll run you through the drill." The therapist had recommended he ask various questions to sidetrack her mind when her fears were at their worst. They usually worked a treat.

"One second." She nabbed the sat phone from the bedside table and clutched it against her chest. Chopper blades whirred overhead, and Saria tipped her ear toward the sound as the craft that had brought him in returned out over the ocean with her sister.

Holding her close, he played with her hair, winding long strands around his finger. She had the most glorious locks, so long they touched her tiny waist. "Breathe slowly in and slowly out. Then tell me all about your favorite place."

"That's being anywhere with you and Lydia." She nestled her cheek against his chest, her breath pulsing in a heated rhythm across his skin. His tension eased. "For a few minutes, I had that. Now she's gone."

"She's coming back, and if you don't have her, you'll always have me. No matter what distance separates us, if you need me, I'm here."

"I love how you're holding me. I used to dream about how it would feel. The reality is so much better." She slid her hand around his waist, stroked his hip. "And I'm supposed to be propositioning you, not blubbering like a baby."

"Propositioning is bad. Blubbering is good."

"That's not what you said a second ago. Propositioning will take my mind off my sister." She tiptoed her fingers closer to his cock.

"So will sleep." His balls tightened and his shaft hardened and jabbed her wrist. "Ignore that." He should be able to control his own body.

"I can't." She looked deep into his eyes as she caressed his length. "You feel so good."

"You're pouncing again." His good intentions were about to

fly right out the window. "I don't have any condoms, Saria, and I'm not taking your virginity, or losing mine."

"I'm protected. During my last medical, I got the hormonal injection."

"I've already explained my position."

"I want you to touch me."

"No." He shook his head, even as his hand betrayed him. He traced her full lower lip, desperate to kiss her properly.

"I want to know what it's like to be with you. What if you gave me one night?"

"Is that your proposition?"

"Yes, and I don't see what we could possibly have to lose by coming to such an agreement. One night is not a relationship."

No, it wasn't, and this need to be with her would continue to rage unless he gave into it.

"Give me twenty-four hours, Ben."

"This is rather sudden."

"After thirty-two years, and months of us sleeping together, you're calling my offer sudden?" She giggled. "That's hysterical."

He leaned in, brushed his lips over hers and tasted her happiness.

"Now that's a start. Seal the deal with another kiss, and I'll give you twenty-four hours of hot sex, even though I have no idea how to do that."

He chuckled, beyond tempted. One day, and no commitment. Every man's dream, and certainly his. His resolve slid away. "I want my own personal game of strip poker."

"You've got it."

His cock hardened further and he allowed his true desire its head. With his mouth lowered to hers, he urged her lips apart, and from one heart-stopping breath to the next, gave himself over to the need that had raged within him for so long. He caressed her sides, roamed down and scooped her bottom.

"Is that a deal?" She seized his arms and clung to him.

"Yes, because it's impossible to say no to you. But if you change your mind, say the word and I'll stop." He kissed her again, so deeply their breath mingled as one and did crazy things to his thoughts. She was the only woman he'd ever wanted. Now he was about to get his wish. One day, with the chance to learn her body so he no longer craved her. The perfect answer to his dreams.

* * * *

Saria clawed Ben closer. He was actually kissing her, and about to do so much more.

"We'll take things slowly," he murmured. "You'll tell me what you like, or what you don't like. What you'd prefer for me to do, or not do."

With painstaking slowness, he grazed a finger along the gap between her yellow sleep-shorts and singlet tee. Her tummy tensed in expectation. "Nothing is off limits, except stopping."

"So I can touch you wherever I please?" He rolled her top up, exposed her entire midriff then bent his head. His warm breath sizzled across her skin and sent an equally delicious heat pulsing through her core.

"Everywhere will please me. Can I touch you too?" She sank her fingers into his tousled blond hair and gasped as he licked around her belly button.

"Yes, please." He nipped in a line upward until his nose brushed the underside of her breasts. He cupped one mound through her thin top and thumbed the peaking tip. "I want to taste every inch of you."

"Ditto."

He sucked her nipple, drawing both it and the cloth into his mouth. Hot. Then he caught her hand, turned it over and kissed her palm in the sweetest caress. Her heart melted as he lifted his gaze to her and smiled. "The sat phone's ringing."

"What?" Oh, heck it was, and it must be her sister. How on earth had she forgotten about Lydia's promised call? The sat phone buzzed and vibrated on the bed. She snatched it up, a whole lot out of breath as she answered, "Hey, did you land already?"

"Sure did. We're all safe and sound." The chopper's blades whirred down in a gentle hum in the background.

"Sorry to make you call, but it really—" She gasped as Ben stroked down the center of her neck and between the valley of her breasts where her top dipped. A seriously hungry look lit his eyes.

"But really what, sis?" Lydia asked.

Ben swept her bodice to the side then eased his hand inside. Grinning, he filled his palm with her flesh. "So beautifully soft. I've never felt the like before." One dark, sexy tone.

"Saria, is that Ben? He's never felt the like of what before?"

She dragged her thoughts back to her sister. "Yes, it's Ben, and he's never felt a woman's breast before."

"What?" A tapping echoed down the line as if Lydia rapped on the earpiece. "I think there's something wrong with this connection. I swear you just said Ben and breast in the same sentence. That can't be right."

"Got to taste you." He licked her nipple, so sensuously slow. "That's good, real good."

"Who's got to taste what, sis?" Lydia asked.

"Apparently me, and I really have to go before my bodyguard gets to have all the fun and I miss out. I'll talk to you when you get back and explain this rambling conversation later." She hung up, tossed the phone onto the bedside table and rose into his exquisite touch. "Getting hot and heavy with you is my best idea yet."

"I totally agree." He drew her aureole deep into his mouth and played the tip with his tongue. Oh, he knew exactly how to use his mouth. She palmed the back of his head and held him against her breast as he razzed her nipple with his teeth.

"That feels amazing. Where did you learn to do that?"

"I may have watched some interesting movies in my time." He tugged her onto her side, gripped the thin strap over her raised shoulder and slid it down her arm until her breast plopped fully free. He wriggled her top down on her other side, all the way to her waist until he'd exposed all of her. "Your breasts are so beautiful and full."

"My turn." She eased his boxers down, encircled her hand around his thick cock and smiled as a drop beaded and glistened on the plump head. "I've watched a few interesting movies myself. Nothing too outlandish, but I do know what I want." She slithered down, licked the tip then swirled her tongue around it. He tasted heavenly, salty and strong, and she sucked, taking as much of him in as she could. Satisfaction hummed through her. She had him for the next twenty-four hours, and she didn't intend to miss the treasure that would be all hers.

He moaned and rocked his hips. "So good."

"If I'm not doing something right, then tell me." She took him deeper, slid her hand lower and cupped his balls covered with a smattering of pale hair. She carefully caressed them.

"You have a wicked mouth, but one I want on mine. Otherwise I'm going to come before we even get started." He pulled her up, tumbled her onto her back and kissed her.

With their bodies locked tight together, he swept his tongue over hers. His hunger was potent, storming through her and building her own.

"Saria, I want to touch you as you just touched me." He gave the hem of her sleep-shorts a tug. "I need to hear a yes."

"Yes. I want this. I want you." She'd tell him that as often as he needed.

"I want you too." He slid his fingers under her waistband, dragged the shorts down and slid her red panties off. His breath caught. "Sweet heaven, you're bare."

"I took care of things down there since my bikini bottoms are a little on the delicate side."

"I like. A lot." He spread her legs and revealed all of her to his hungry gaze. With the softest touch, he stroked a finger over her skin then down her slit. "So wet."

She slid her legs against his, her heartbeat a pounding mess. Then he ducked his head and she tangled her hands in his golden hair. She held onto him as his tongue swept across her flesh. A firestorm radiated out from where he touched, and then he moved his mouth over her sensitive clit, and sucked.

"You must have watched those movies with dedicated attention."

"I've fantasized about this, how you would taste, even though I never considered doing anything about it." Licking her, he built her orgasm to exquisite perfection.

"Fantasies are good, particularly if I'm on the receiving end." She lifted her hips and her legs fell wider.

"Yes, but reality is even better." He grasped her bottom, drank from her deeper and moaned. "Hell, my cock is about to burst. I don't think I can hold on much longer."

"Then don't." She clutched him to her. "Please, I want you inside me."

"It will hurt, and I can't take that pain away." He rose over her. "I wish I had more experience to offer you, but I'll do everything I can to make this good."

"I trust you, and if we do this wrong, neither of us will really know."

He grinned, nipped her lower lip, and then with his hands on her hips, he slowly, carefully, moved between her legs and nudged his cock along her slick folds.

She cupped his face, looked into his eyes. "Whatever you do, don't stop."

"I couldn't even if I wanted to." He pushed against the barrier, tore through and plunged deep inside. Her gasp was muffled against his neck as she held on. Carefully, he eased up then gently pushed back in. "Does this feel uncomfortable?"

"More like very full."

"This feels incredible, like every nerve ending in my body is charged and sparking where we touch." He moved in and out, stroking into her slow and easy.

"It feels good for me too." Her lashes fluttered down. "Real good."

"Don't close your eyes." He increased his pace, pounding harder. "I want to see your pleasure when it comes."

She opened her eyes. He was buried so exquisitely deep, and his heartbeat thumped against hers. Then he laid claim to her lips and sent every one of her last thoughts flying. "Touch me below. So close," she murmured.

"Here?" He caressed her clit, and she cried his name. Her inner muscles tightened and locked him in place. Blissful spasm after spasm racked her body as he stroked with the sweetest touch. He'd taken her over, as she'd known he would.

"I love how you feel coming around me." He drove deep then jerked, his seed shooting inside her, and with the skill of his mouth taking hers, he sent her careening again over the edge and into complete oblivion.

He collapsed on top, still buried deep in her heat.

For this moment, he was hers, and she wrapped her arms around his neck and held onto him.

* * * *

A buzz of pleasure continued to vibrate through Ben's body well after his release. His heart still pumped at warp speed, but then so did Saria's in the most chaotic rhythm against his. He should pull out, but he wanted to stay locked inside her body, to saturate himself in her warmth and not relinquish her heavenly hold.

He kissed her neck, and her answering purr soothed his soul. "Are you okay?"

"Never better." She claimed his mouth, her kiss a slow exploration that left him breathless and dizzy for more.

"I want to get lost inside you." His cock twitched and he ached to move, to rock deeper, only the smear of blood on her thighs proved she must be hurting. Carefully, he lifted onto his elbows and slid out.

"Where are you going?"

"I don't want to hurt you any more than I have. How about a shower? We've both made a bit of a mess."

"Okay, I am feeling rather sticky." She wriggled out of her top still bunched around her waist.

After easing off the bed, he took her hand and walked with her into her private bathroom with its pale floor tiles, cream vanity and fluffy blue towels. Touching her so freely invigorated him. For so long, he'd withheld.

"You have the silliest grin on your face." She rubbed her cheek against his shoulder. "What are you thinking?"

"That I waited for you, as sappy as that sounds." He opened the glass shower door and flicked the water on.

"I like that." Saria skipped inside then tipped her head back under the spray. The water sluiced through her brown locks, sending strands sliding over her breasts. She squirted shampoo into her hand and washed her hair. "Dip your head into the water. I'll do you too."

No one had ever washed his hair for him, but he did as she'd asked and enjoyed every moment as she massaged the shampoo in. After rinsing it out, he picked up the bar of soap, lathered and smoothed the suds down her sides, around her back and over her lower cheeks.

"You have magic hands, a magic mouth, and tongue. In case you'd like to know."

"I've heard the first time for a girl can be more painful than pleasurable." He lowered to his knees, rubbed the suds over her belly and mound. "Spread your legs and I'll take care of you here as well."

"You're always taking care of me." She widened her stance, and he glided the soap along the inside of her thighs until she shivered and gripped his shoulders. "Which I really like."

He liked to. "Pass me the shower head. I'll be gentle."

"I know you will." She unhooked and handed it over, her trust in him as unwavering as ever.

Running warm water over her folds, he cleaned her then passed the showerhead back, and with her flesh still parted, softly kissed her. "You're clean." He rose to his feet.

"I think it might pay for me to watch those movies you watched. My turn." She soaped his balls and shaft as carefully and tenderly as he'd done with her.

"Time for bed, and I mean sleep." He wanted to get dirty all over again, but shut the water off, swiped a towel from the rail and wrapped it around her. He nabbed the other for himself.

Yawning, she tottered back to the bedroom. From the caramel-painted dresser, she selected pink lace panties and a silk cami. Just as well he'd never known what kind of sexy underwear Saria wore under her pajamas.

He foraged in his duffel for another pair of boxers, donned them and joined her in bed. The gap between them, which he'd always ensured, had now become the widest chasm. "Can I hold you?"

"If you don't, you're in trouble." She snuggled under his shoulder, draped one arm around his waist and curled her leg over his. Her breath caressed his chest as she drifted.

Finally, he was able to hold her, and nothing had ever soothed him more.

He drifted, allowing sleep to claim him.

Chapter 3

Afternoon sunshine slithered between two of the pale blue blinds, which had snagged and not quite overlapped. The light streamed over Saria's closed eyelids and she blinked and stretched. Muscles she'd never used before ached, but in the best way. Beside her, Ben snoozed, his silky blond hair a rumpled mess and his jaw holding a razz of golden stubble.

Overhead, the distinct whirr of chopper blades drummed then passed toward the resort and faded. Hopefully Lydia and Tyler were back. Eager to check and not sleep her entire first day in the islands away, she snuck out of bed, snagged her denim cutoffs and a lacy yellow-paneled top from the dresser and raced to the bathroom. Dressed, her teeth cleaned and her hair fastened in a high ponytail, she added a smear of lippy and tiptoed back to the bedroom.

Ben had rolled onto his front and lay sprawled across both sides of the bed, his arms crossed under his cheek. The position stretched his broad shoulders and with the sheet pooled at his hips, showed off his muscular back and trim waist. Her mouth watered at the tempting display.

How she wanted to stay, but she needed to make sure Lydia was okay. She picked up the sat phone and forced herself to walk out of the room. After closing the door with a gentle snick, she strolled down the plush-carpeted cream passageway. Halogen lights beamed over vivid blue underwater ocean scenes adorning the length of the caramel-cream walls.

She wandered up the winding stairs to the second floor. Outside the open double glass lounge doors, the crystal blue water beckoned, and beyond, the resort's white and blue striped sun umbrellas dotting the beach provided shade for families lazing on colorful towels beneath them.

For the first time in what felt like forever, the tension she'd carried in her muscles finally eased away. Ben was close, safe and well, and she could sense her sister's closeness through their twin bond. Lydia had been on that chopper.

"Hey, you're up and awake. Did you have a good sleep?" Dylan waved from the long oak dining table past the cozy groupings of four white leather couches. At twenty-seven, Dylan had risen through the ranks of Whitehall Shipping and earned the position of chief engineer, and as she'd learnt yesterday, he played a very analytical game of poker.

"I did. Thanks for asking." Her rubber-soled sandals squelched as she crossed the polished pine floors. She plopped onto the padded chair beside him. "Where is everyone?"

"Liam and Nico have gone sandcastle building. Luke took his surfboard out to the where the waves are rolling in the sweetest, and Brigs is still napping. I take it Ben is too?"

"He's completely out of it." She set the sat phone on the table.

"How are you feeling?" He kicked out his long legs clad in beige cargo shorts and crossed them at the ankle.

"Ben's here, so much better." She smiled as her thoughts returned to the man who'd made love to her so passionately. "My fears have eased, and I'm not going to let them rear up again. I'm even going to take a walk. It'll be my first out on my own in a year without a bodyguard looming over me."

"I can come if you'd like, and I promise no looming."

"Thanks, but I need to do this alone." On its white lace

doily, she slid the center fruit bowl closer. Bunches of purple and green grapes were nestled around juicy peaches and apricots. She plucked a grape, popped it into her mouth and moaned as its sweet juice exploded over her tongue. Delicious.

"I'll drop that sat phone back in the control room if you'd like. I'm heading up to see the captain shortly." Dylan selected a banana hiding on the other side of the bowl and peeled it. "Where are you headed on your walk? There's a ton to see."

"To the pharmacy if there is one." It wouldn't hurt to grab some additional protection since her hormonal injection was due again soon.

"There's one inside the main building, tucked on the lower level next to the doctor's clinic."

"There's a clinic?" Fantastic. She'd make an appointment with the doctor instead. She selected a peach then strolled to the door. "In case Ben wakes up looking for me, tell him I'll be back before it gets dark." Which was early in the tropics, about six. She'd have a couple of hours tops.

"You enjoy your walk."

"I will." She breathed deep as she crossed the deck and walked down the gangplank onto the wharf. The salty sea breeze ticked her nose and recharged her senses. Now this was life, and she was finally living it again.

"Well, look at you, Miss Independent." Lydia, dressed in a short floral island skirt and pale pink shirt, released Tyler's hand and bounced toward her. "Outside, and without a chaperone. I'm so proud of you."

"I feel exhilarated, and my chaperone's asleep. Having you and Ben back is exactly what I needed to get back to being my old self. How was your trip? All licensed up?"

"Almost. We have to return to pick up the completed paperwork in three days. They have to run checks, make sure we're who we say we are and all that jazz. But less about me. You need to explain that strange conversation earlier, because you wouldn't believe the thoughts going through my head."

"Mine too." Tyler, his dark hair newly trimmed, cocked a brow as he joined them. "I've known Ben since we bunked together in the barracks. I've never seen him date a woman, not in all this time."

"You never asked him why?"

"I figured it was personal."

"Men. You live by a different set of rules to us." Such a shame he didn't know. Some insider information on her elusive bodyguard would have been helpful.

"Yes, but you and I don't live by those rules." Lydia nudged her. "Spill."

"Not much to spill. Ben's definitely not into relationships, so we've agreed to some fun." The wind blew her hair across her face and she tucked it behind her ears.

"Fun is good." Lydia nodded. "And Ben couldn't be more trustworthy. So where are you off to?"

"The doctor's office. Thought I'd get a quick checkup."

"Did you want me to come?"

"I want to take a walk on my own and finish tossing those unnecessary fears of mine aside."

"Great, then go forth, demolish and destroy."

"Tyler is rubbing off on you. I'll catch you later." She chuckled and bit into her peach.

Foamy waves rolled in and beat against the thick round pillar posts as she walked on, a soothing swish that further settled her. Seagulls squawked overhead as they circled for fish and the delighted squeals of children playing in the surf rang in her ears. Her fears continued to settle. Yes, the Hyena brothers who'd been after her and Lydia had both been caught. Mia Taita, the orchestrator behind the contract to take Lydia out, was behind bars with them. This was a regular day, without any killers or maniacs in sight. Justice was being served. She and her sister were finally free to live again.

After marching up the beach, she followed the winding coral sandstone path through the resort's tropical gardens. Dozens of holidaymakers swam in the three sprawling pools while others relaxed on the surrounding white canvas loungers.

Staff behind the pool bar counter served colorful drinks with cute little umbrellas, and a DJ played music from a nearby coconut frond-roofed shack. Perfect, and so relaxing. She tossed her peach pip into the waste bin then wandered toward the main four-story building ahead.

She trod across a bridged walkway spanning a pond of floating lily pads and croaking frogs. A boy, maybe six or seven, tossed scraps of bread into the water and a swarm of orange and yellow goldfish darted to the surface and gobbled the food.

Three girls darted past to watch the fish feeding and knocked her against the side rail in their haste. She clutched the wooden balustrade.

"Watch out." A uniformed cleaner pushing a trolley of towels and mops ran into her from behind.

"Ouch." She grabbed her ankle and hopped on one foot.

"Miss, I'm so sorry." The woman raced around and gasped, one hand over her mouth. "Oh, you're bleeding."

"It's okay." And nothing close to having a murderer chasing her. Although her ankle stung along the jagged edge of the inch long cut. "Do you have a first aid kit?"

"Right here somewhere." Tossing starched white linens, she foraged through her trolley.

"Are you all right? I'm Dr. Hika." A middle-aged dark-skinned man in a crisp cream shirt and tailored beige shorts stopped and hunkered down to inspect her wound. His black springy hair flopped forward over his brow.

"I'm Saria Sands, and I'll be fine once this gets covered up." Great. Her first trip out and she'd gotten jittery and hurt herself.

"Here it is." The cleaner pulled a small red plastic container out of her trolley and passed it to the doctor. "My first aid kit. This is all my fault."

"No, it's mine too," she assured the woman. "It's not like you were able to stop your cart in time. I'm a nurse. I can handle a little blood."

"Don't you worry. I'll sort this." The doctor nodded at the cleaner then caught Saria's elbow. "Are you okay to walk to that bench over there? We need to clear the bridge so others can get by, then I can see to your injury."

"Yes, and thank you." Trying not to drip blood on the wooden planks, she hopped with his aid across to a slatted seat beside the pond and sat.

"Sorry, we do try not to harm the tourists visiting our fair land. I particularly don't like seeing nurses in distress. Are you hurt anywhere else other than your ankle?" The doctor popped the lid on the kit, selected a cotton ball and smeared it with antiseptic cream. He wiped the wound then applied a thick plaster. "You were holding your hip."

"I knocked into the railing." She rubbed her side. "It's fine. No harm done there."

"You seem a little pale."

"It's my first time out in a while. The cleaner gave me a fright. That's all. I was on my way to make an appointment with you."

"Sorry, I have no idea when my next opening is. My nurse is currently away and the receptionist at the pharmacy now takes my bookings. In the meantime, let's make sure you can walk without any issue." He took her elbow and helped her up. "There's a meadow close by, and I can guarantee it's free of any wayward trolleys. This way."

She limped along the meandering garden path that veered away toward the rear where the jungle rose thick and lush beyond the resort. Bright red and pink flowering hibiscus bushes dotted the gardens surrounding the grassy meadow. Across the far side, several children played a game of tag while a uniformed caregiver in the resort's yellow skirt and polo supervised.

Two teens in shorts and t-shirts volleyed a ball between them. One kicked it so hard it sailed over her head and clunked into something metal within the bushes, an abandoned gardening shed by the looks.

"Sorry," the boy called out to her as he scrambled through the brush. He grabbed his ball out of the ivy trailing over the shed's door then tossed it back to his friend.

"This is lovely." She could handle a flying ball, and her ankle might have taken a knock, but she could walk with only a pinch of pain. "It's good for me to be out and around others. I've had a rather secluded year of late, and it's caused a few fears to rise."

"Nothing too debilitating I hope."

"I get a big jumpy if someone comes up behind me. The cleaner truly wouldn't have run into me if I hadn't jumped in her path first, and now my bodyguard has arrived, I'm hoping my fears will soon be well and truly done with." She plucked a yellow buttercup at her feet and twirled it between two fingers. "This island is certainly the perfect place to begin healing."

"You need a bodyguard?"

"Not anymore I don't."

"Well, at least you're walking without any issue. I'd hate to get on the wrong side of your bodyguard, whether you need him or not."

"The plaster's working a real treat."

He grinned. "Yes, the old plaster fixes all."

"Hey, Saria." Luke jostled through a tight beachside path barely noticeable with its thick hedge either side. He jogged toward her in red swim trunks, his surfboard tucked under one arm. He shook his dark head and sent water flying. "I caught a glimpse of you as I came out of the water. I was about to head back to the ship." He propped his board beside him, and its long shadow fell across the doctor's face.

"You've got great eyesight." Only a peek of the ocean was viewable, although the crashing of the waves reached her easily on the breeze. "Meet Dr. Hika. He rescued me from a trolley and bandaged me up. Dr. Hika, this is Luke Whitehall. Luke's family, or he will be soon. We're here for my twin sister and his brother's wedding."

"Nice to meet you, Luke." The doctor extended his hand and Luke shook it. "How are the waves today?"

"Sweet, although I don't know how you concentrate on getting any work done when you have all this in your backyard." Luke patted his surfboard's bright blue swirling ocean design.

"Trust me. It's difficult." The doctor's cell phone buzzed and he checked the display. "Sorry. It appears my free time is up. My next appointment beckons." He glanced at her. "Saria, you'll find the pharmacy on the first floor when you go to make your appointment. Enjoy your day." He waved as he walked away.

"Do you want to explain a trolley on the run?" Luke eyed her ankle. "I see the bandage."

"Plaster, and the doctor's appointment isn't for this minor injury. Do you want to walk me back to the ship though? I think I've had enough sightseeing for one day." Making an appointment could wait.

"Of course I will." He slotted his surfboard back under his arm and guided her toward the gap in the trees.

She shuffled through the overgrown path and gasped as they made the beach. Only one lone sunbather was sprawled on a towel catching the last of the day's rays. "This is nice and private."

"Yeah, it's one of my favorite places."

"How often do you sail this way?" They strolled down the beach.

"Three or four times a year. After we lost Mum, and Liam and Nico lost Gabriella, it became even more important for us to connect as a family." He led the way onto the wharf. "Liam loves taking Nico sandcastle building. It reminds him of how Gabriella adored doing the same when Nico was a toddler."

"That's a beautiful way to keep the memories alive, for both of them." Her heart ached for Liam and Nico's loss.

Next to their yacht, another of a similar length and four-level height, had berthed. Ben raced past it toward them, his blue gaze fixed on her. Outfitted in black shorts and a shirt, his blond hair whipped about his shoulders in the breeze. She grinned. "You're up."

"And you should have woken me when you decided to come outside." He stopped in front of her, hands on his hips.

"You were out of it." She linked her arm through the crook in his.

"Dylan said you were taking a look around."

"I didn't get very far." She stepped on board, wandered downstairs and into her room.

"Why is your foot bandaged?" He shut the door.

"It's my ankle, and it's a plaster."

"That doesn't explain how you got hurt."

"I got nicked by the cleaner's trolley." On her tiptoes, she kissed his chin. "I met the resident doctor. A very nice man."

"For a simple cut?" He appeared so serious, his brow creased and his gaze as watchful as ever.

"Yes, they've got exceptional service around here. He even took a walk with me and made sure I hadn't suffered any lasting injuries." She kicked off her sandals, plopped down on the leather couch and rested her head on the decorative blue pillow. "How was your sleep?"

"Lonely toward the end." Ben lifted her feet, eased in beside her and set them back on his lap. He stroked her calves. "Though I had an extraordinary dream."

"Want to share?" She crossed her arms behind her head.

"I imagined you on your hands and knees beneath me, your

back to my front as I slid right into you." He skimmed one hand over her knee and along her outer thigh. His eyelids lowered and his breath came harder. So did hers.

"Well then, next time I'll let the cleaner ram her trolley into someone else and I'll stay and play out your dream with you."

"We could play now if you want? We did agree on an entire day." He smoothed around to her inner thigh, his roaming touch setting her pulse fluttering below. "How sore are you?" He flicked the hem of her lacy yellow-paneled top up and exposed her midriff. Gently, he traced her belly button, his gaze on hers.

"I'm aching"—she lifted her leg and slid her toes over his crotch—"for some of this package you've got on the rise."

"I also dream of seeing you ride me." He spanned her waist, his fingertips grazing the underside of her breasts. Slowly he lifted her and straddled her across his lap. "Do you think that would be possible for us to play that dream out too?"

"You don't even need to ask." Wanting and prepared to fulfill all of his dreams, she leaned in and kissed him.

* * * *

"I take it that's a yes?" Unlike his father, Ben would never take a woman by force. Which meant he needed to hear Saria's complete agreement, no matter her actions spoke louder than words.

"Let me see." She unbuttoned his black shirt, separated the material and pressed her mouth against his flat nipple. She sucked, and a deep coil of longing flared inside him.

"Answer me." He pressed her head tighter to his chest. If she said no, he was sunk.

"Yes. My breasts even throb when I kiss you like this." She razzed her teeth over the tip as he'd done to her nipples that morning. "I'm getting very wet."

He shoved a hand under her shirt and cupped her bare breast. Damn, she'd gone out without a bra. She better be wearing panties. He popped the dome on her denim shorts, slid the zipper down and smoothed his fingertips over her satin underwear.

"I want to ride you, be underneath you, or any other position you fantasize about. If you can imagine it, I'm in."

At her words, lust shot straight to his cock and it rose and speared into her bottom.

"Nice." She wriggled against him. "I see you like sexy talk."

"I like anything you have to say." He pinched her nipple, and she pushed deeper into his hand.

"Do that again, or kiss me. Either works."

He kissed her, ravishing her mouth as he wished to ravish the rest of her. In a heartbeat he toppled her onto the couch, dragged her shorts down her slim legs and off. "I really like these pink panties, but they have to go. All of your clothes do."

"Yours need to as well." On her back, she wriggled her panties off then tugged her shirt over her head. "Now, Hammers."

"I love it when you say my name like that." He shucked his shorts and got rid of his shirt. The setting sun's reds and pinks coming through the wide window bathed her body. Her breasts were full, the tips hard, and his tongue tingled for another taste. Lower still, her bare mound beckoned with the ultimate prize hidden within. "I need to get my fill of you, Saria."

"I thought you wanted me to ride you."

"That too, but I need other things first." Blood pounding, he lowered his head and kissed her, allowing the temptation of her mouth to consume him. Saria held a potent appeal he couldn't resist. She was sweet, fiery, and incredibly passionate.

"I want your hands on me, everywhere." She rubbed her chest against his and her nipples, so incredibly hard, scraped across his flesh. "I never want to forget this day."

Neither did he. And the way she looked at him, with such longing and trust, seared his soul.

Plundering her breasts, he rolled one tip while he licked the other. He teased his teeth over her nipple then pulled it deep inside his mouth. His cock hardened further until the exquisite pressure below bordered on painful.

He kissed down her body to where her folds glistened. Definitely wet. Revealing more of her, he gripped her legs and spread them. She'd never be able to hide herself from him. "You're so beautiful, Saria. I want to make you come, over and over."

"Slow down." She tangled her hands in his hair and held onto him. Her possessive grip soothed him, but slowed him down not one bit. He ducked his head and lashed her flesh. She wrapped her legs around him as she thrashed underneath. "Please, I don't want to come without you."

He clasped her hips then slowly moved his cock between her legs. Sliding himself along her folds, he lubricated himself with her slickness. "You want me here?"

"Yes, we'll get to the other stuff you dream about later. Make me yours." She clutched his butt and pulled him inside her.

"You'll never be anyone else's." He kissed her, pounding hard. Her soft moans encouraged him, and he took her frantically, unable to hold back.

"Ben." She raked his back as she cried his name.

"I'm right here." He was lost as her inner muscles tightened and dragged him home. His thoughts flew and his release exploded violently along with hers. Deep within, he spilled himself until she'd wrung him dry.

With no strength remaining, he collapsed.

A more perfect moment, he'd never known.

She was his.

Chapter 4

Saria lay on the padded couch, Ben a delicious weight on top of her. His body was hard and packed with muscle, his shoulders and arms thick and strong. She blew gently over the light sheen of his sweat-dampened skin. "Ben, wake up."

"Too heavy?" His voice was a mumble as he stirred.

"Yes, but in a wonderful way. I don't want you to move."

He eased up onto his elbows and looked into her eyes, so focused, in a way he'd never been before.

She wanted to kiss him, to make him hers forever.

"What are you thinking?" He stroked her cheek.

"That making love to you is very special."

His cock twitched and lengthened inside her. "Say that again and we'll soon get round two underway."

"I want round two." Did she ever.

"Saria." A knock sounded on the door.

"Argh, my sister has the worst timing." To Lydia, she yelled, "Don't come in. I'm not decent, and neither is the sexy man lying on top of me."

"If you're not decent, I'm staying right here," Lydia called back. "Dinner is served and you're expected upstairs. That's if you can extricate yourself from the so-called sexy man. Talk to you both soon." She giggled and her footsteps faded away.

"We should join the others." Ben nipped her lips. "You use

the bathroom first, because if I'm in there with you, we'll never leave the room." He eased out of her then took her hands and helped her to her feet.

"Sure, but I expect more time with you later. You have dreams I want to explore, over and over." She claimed a quick kiss then with an extra swing to her hips, sauntered into the bathroom. She searched the vanity's top drawer, grabbed her wide-tooth comb and brushed out the frightful mess having fun with Ben made to her hair. She set a clip at each side, gold with a twinkling diamond, the set identical to one Lydia had too. Done, she opened the door and leaned naked against the bedroom wall. Ben wore black dress pants and a sky-blue shirt, his golden locks curling over the collar. "The bathroom's all yours."

"Thank you." Rolling his shirtsleeves to the elbow, he strode past her and shut the door. From the other side, he muttered, "Make damn sure you're dressed when I come back out, otherwise no food for you."

"That's hardly a threat." She wriggled into a short white summer dress. Knotted lightly around the neck, the cotton ties tickled her back and made her feel as sexy as hell. Or that could have been the heated look in Ben's blue eyes just moments ago when he'd passed her by.

Ben stepped out of the bathroom, clean-shaven and looking completely edible. She certainly wouldn't mind taking a bite out of him. Instead, she slipped on five-inch racy-red heels and walked out of the room with her bodyguard one step behind.

"The back of that dress is quite low. One would think you're not wearing a bra again."

"I'm not."

He stumbled and thumped into the wall. "Damn, I'm never going to get through dinner without laying my hands on you."

"I don't have panties on either, and you can lay your hands on me whenever and wherever you like." At his fierce groan, she skipped upstairs, her heels clicking loudly across the polished wooden floors.

Liam, the eldest, sat at the head of the long oak dining table with Nico on a pillowed seat tucked in beside him. Dylan, Luke and Brigs, all dressed in slacks and dark dinner shirts, were seated along one side while Tyler and Lydia sat opposite.

Ben pulled out the chair next to Lydia for her.

"Sorry we're late, everyone." He took the end seat then stretched out his legs and touched this tips of his black leather shoes to hers.

"Better late than never." Tyler raised a brow at Ben. "I also understand the difficulty of getting ready in time when there's a distracting woman in sight."

"Difficulty?" Lydia shoved her elbow into his arm and sent the yellow ruffles of her short dress's scalloped neckline fluttering. "Please, you'd keep me locked in our bedroom if you could, and I'd never get to eat."

"And therein lies the problem."

"Excuse me, sir," Henry dipped his head toward Tyler. "Is everyone ready to eat?"

"Yes thanks, Henry. Bring in the dishes."

"Certainly, sir." He clapped.

The swinging galley door opened and the wait staff swished through. They wandered around the table and set dinner plates down. The succulent aroma of pan-fried fish stacked on top of roasted sweet potato and kumara, had Saria licking her lips. Nico squealed and Liam picked up his son's knife and fork and cut his meat for him, while across from her, Dylan and Luke thanked the servers.

Brigs frowned as he glanced at Ben. "What am I missing? What distracting woman do you have in your sight?"

"None at all." Ben clapped Brigs on the shoulder. "As usual, you sleep too much."

"Brigs." Lydia plunked her elbows on the table and cleared her throat. "I have a favor to ask. Saria and I need to shop for dresses, ones I don't want any men to see."

"Why don't I like the sound of this?" He bit into his fish.

"Tomorrow, I need you to keep Tyler busy while Saria and I take the chopper to the mainland. Perhaps you can take Tyler and Ben fishing. Guy stuff, you know."

"Hold on." Tapping his knife on the tabletop, Ben glared at Lydia. "You two aren't going to the mainland alone."

"Yes, we are." Lydia reached past Saria and patted Ben's hand. "You're used to guarding us, but that time has come to an end. There's no reason why Saria and I can't shop on our own."

Tyler growled under his breath. "I'm not sure I'm prepared for you to go it alone. Too many people were trying to kill you just last week. I can still hear the blast of gunshots in my ears."

"Both Kern and Ladd Hyena are in jail," Lydia countered, "and so is Mia Taita who contracted them to come after us."

"I still don't like it."

"Neither do I," Ben gritted out.

"I'm not asking either of you if you like it, but Saria and I need to move on. We have a life to live, and shopping is usually a harmless activity." Lydia turned her sweetest smile on Brigs. "You'll do this for me, won't you?"

"You're a cruel woman, but yes, I'm up for the challenge."

"Fishing and guy stuff probably won't cut it, Brigs," Tyler grunted. "I'll need a major distraction."

Saria stabbed a cube of roasted potato with her fork and chewed. "I think Lydia's right. It'll be good for us to go to the mainland alone. I'm looking forward to it."

"Great. I'll order the chopper since it's all settled." Lydia passed Tyler her glass of water. "Take a drink."

"I'll need something stronger than that if I'm going to make it through tomorrow." He grabbed his glass of white wine and took a hearty gulp.

"I still don't like this." Ben squeezed her leg under the table.

"We'll be fine." Saria leaned in and whispered in his ear, "It's that codependency rearing its head again."

"I don't care. It doesn't feel right having you two go off on your own."

"That doesn't mean it's wrong."

She settled back as around her, the others chatted and the conversation moved on. The wait staff continued to fill their glasses, and after the first course, they returned with dessert and set plates before them. Each held a generous slice of chocolate mud cake with fresh raspberries and cream. Delicious. After she'd finished, she wanted to lick her plate clean.

Ben polished off his dessert and she wiped a smear of cream from the corner of his lips then licked her finger. His gaze zeroed in on her mouth, his hungry thoughts blatantly clear to see.

"Would you like to take a walk after dinner?" she asked him.

"Would that walk be downstairs?"

"That'd be my preference."

"Mine too." He caught the back of her head, brought her closer and kissed her. "Sorry, couldn't help myself."

"Shoot." Brigs's breath whistled out. "That's something I didn't think I'd ever see. Are you two together?"

"Yes." Ben frowned. "I mean no."

"Come on, sis." Lydia, finished with her dessert, scraped her chair back. "I want you to take a walk with me before Ben distracts you for the rest of the night. I also want to hear all the juicy details of, well, whatever you've been up to lately."

Tyler and Ben both groaned. Yeah, nothing was ever off limits when they talked and the men knew it.

They wandered down the gangplank and onto the wharf. Her sister unstrapped her heels and she followed suit. Leaving their shoes next to their mooring, they stepped onto the sand still warm from the day's heat. The breeze cooled her skin, and the frothy-tipped waves rolled into shore and splashed her feet.

"I've missed these kinds of moments." Lydia linked arms with her and let out a contented sigh. "Now, tell me everything. Is Ben pushing all the right buttons?"

"Yes, but we agreed on button-pushing for one day and no more." She cleared her throat. "I want to share something with you but you need to keep it to yourself, okay?"

"I love a secret, and I promise not to say a word." She crossed her heart.

"Like me, Ben was a virgin."

"No way." Lydia's brown eyes went wide. "I know Tyler said he'd never even seen Ben date a woman before, but I didn't realize that meant he was into abstinence. Still, that's kinda cool you were each other's first. Do you know why he chose to wait?"

"He said there were bad genes in his family's stock. He has issues, and whatever they are, I'm keener than ever to get to the bottom of them. I certainly understand he doesn't want a relationship, and not everyone does, but I think there's so much more to it than that." They strolled up the sand dune and sat with the coconut trees swishing in the gentle breeze behind them. Across the darkened water, light glowed from behind the ship's slatted blinds.

"Yes, but you two are close. If anyone can get Ben to open up, it would be you. Ah, looky there." Lydia motioned toward the ship where Ben and Tyler emerged from the dining room and walked across to the stern. Tyler leaned against the rail then hand to his brow, peered their way. Lydia waved and checked her watch. "A whole eight minutes. Those boys are slipping."

Saria laughed as the men marched along the wharf toward them. "Poor Brigs. I hate to think how he's going to handle them tomorrow."

"My bet's not very well since they hate not being in control." Lydia shoved to her feet. "Time for you to have some one-on-one time with your man. See if you can't get him to open up about those issues."

"I'll do my best. Thanks for the privacy."

"Anytime, and think interrogation. Grill the man for whatever information you need." Lydia grinned as she strolled toward Tyler, caught his hand then led him back toward the ship.

Ben jogged across, plopped down next to her and linked his hands over his raised knees. "Are you all right?"

"Never better." She slid her hand over the back of his and rubbed a soothing circle over his knuckles. "How are you feeling?"

"Like I need more time alone with you." He brought her hand to his lips and kissed her fingertips. "What did Lydia have to say?"

"She gave me the go ahead to interrogate you."

"That sounds dangerous." He watched the waves rolling in. "About what exactly?"

"Your issues." She brushed a finger along his cheek and gently moved his gaze back to hers. "Tell me about your family. You never speak of them."

"I don't have any family. Raised in the foster system, remember?"

"Yes, but you must know who they are." He had the ability to track them with such ease through his mass of contacts. "Was yours a closed case?"

"No, nothing I ever asked for was withheld from me. I requested my full file when I was thirteen and read all the damning evidence firsthand."

"What evidence?"

"Saria, no." He shook his head. "I've accepted my past and I'd rather it stay right where it is."

"You mean controlling you?"

"Everyone who's ever known the truth has turned away from me." He slapped his legs and stood. "I can't lose you too, which means this conversation is done." He stormed along the beach and into the dark.

"Hey, you're not allowed to run from me." She chased after him. "Wait up, Hammers."

"Go back to the ship, Saria. That's an order."

"You're upset and I won't leave you alone when you're feeling this way." She raced around him then hiked it backward, her hand pressed against his chest. "You also don't have one bad gene in your body. You're a man who has dedicated his life to helping others."

"Yeah, to right the wrongs of my stupid father."

Now she was getting somewhere. "What did your father do to you?"

"Not me. Two days after he was released from the slammer, he raped two eighteen-year-olds. Mary Hammers was one of them, and she had to bear the burden of carrying me." He fisted one hand and punched his other palm. "I'm surprised I ever survived my birth."

She covered his fist with both her hands. "So you feel as if you have to pay for what your father did?"

"My birth should never have happened, which means my ruthless father's line ends with me." He pulled away, strode up the beach and disappeared into the dark interior of the jungle.

An innocent child, not at fault for how he'd been conceived, shouldn't have to pay for the sins of his father. No wonder he'd never told anyone the truth. She ran after him, barely catching the crunch of his step somewhere far ahead.

Low branches scraped her shoulders and face as she stumbled in the pitch black. Prickly bracken stung her bare feet, and whatever moonlight shone above, hadn't a chance of penetrating the dense foliage overhead.

Long minutes passed with no trace of his movement.

She knocked into a trunk, bent and caught her breath. An owl hooted.

"Ben!" She screamed his name. "I need you."

Crashing surf rumbled close, but he didn't reply. She trekked toward the roaring ocean, plowed through the tree line and tumbled down a sand dune onto her bottom. Moonlight trickled over the secluded area scattered with driftwood and seaweed.

Clutching her chest, she willed her racing heartbeat to slow. Ben was safe even though running from his problems. She'd find him. She had to. She controlled her breathing, slowly in and slowly out as the therapist had instructed her if panic set in. With no time to lose, she shoved to her feet and set out in pursuit of her bodyguard.

She'd never abandon him as so many others had done.

He was hers to care for.

* * * *

Arms pumping, Ben ran. Voices played in his head, those of the foster parents he'd been shipped from one to the next from. He was the son of a rapist, a man who deserved to die. They'd pitied him, but pity wouldn't get him anywhere in life. The moment he'd turned eighteen, he'd gotten as far away from anyone who'd ever known the terrible circumstances of his birth as he could. With limited funds, he'd joined the army, and there he'd met Brigs and Tyler. All these years, he'd never spoken a word beyond the bare necessities, and now he'd blabbed every damning detail to Saria. As soon as the knowledge sank in, she too would pity him. He shouldn't have told her.

Exhausted after crossing a mile of jungle, he stumbled through the trees and onto the white sand beach. The stars twinkled above.

At least he was alone, like he'd always been.

He sank onto the sand and fell back.

Hell, he'd done his best to carve out something for himself, even giving up the dream of having a family. No woman should ever have to bear his children knowing they too would face the same ridicule he had while growing up.

"Ben!"

He sat upright.

Saria ran down the beach, her short white dress illuminated by the moonlight and her dark locks swaying around her waist. She appeared a vision, one he wanted to hold onto, but he had to end their time together. Being with her would never work.

"Here," he called out, not wanting her running aimlessly around the island in search of him.

"There you are." She dashed toward him, fell onto her knees then toppled him onto his back as she sprawled over top. "I was so worried. You've never run from me like that before."

"I wasn't running from you, but letting you go."

"Right now, I'm not going anywhere." She kissed him, her breath hot as it mingled with his. "I want every one of those twenty-four hours you promised me."

"Well, you're out of luck." He gripped her arms and instilled some distance, an inch, but one necessary inch. "My father is a rapist, the scum of the earth."

"And you're the exact opposite, my thirty-two-year-old virgin."

"Ex-virgin."

"Which I'm rather pleased about." She kissed him again and he wanted to rip her clothes off and take everything she offered except she would never be his. For her own good, he had to let her go.

"I don't want you, Saria."

"You're not responsible for what your father did, or for your mother's actions when she handed you over into the foster system. I can't even imagine the pain and anguish she must have gone through, but at least she gave you your life, and for that I'll be immensely grateful."

"I said my father was a rapist."

"I heard you the first time, but that doesn't change who you are. You would die to protect me. I know your true heart."

"We'll never be together. The last thing I want is a relationship."

"I understand that's your choice, but before we became lovers, we were friends. If you give me nothing else beyond the day you promised me, I want that friendship back." She rubbed against him, one eyebrow raised as she encountered his hard cock. "See, and that is what I want right now."

The need to make love to her one last time thrummed through him, but it would all be for nothing. "You have your whole life ahead of you, and it's not with me."

"Ah, but until dawn you're all mine, and I've never known you to back out of an agreement." Straddling his hips with her knees in the sand, she pulled the ties on the back of her dress and wriggled the fabric down until the soft cotton pooled at her waist. The cool night air tightened her nipples and made him hunger for more.

"You're using seduction to get your way."

"I certainly will if it works." She pressed her breasts together. "Kiss them. I love feeling your mouth on my body."

Seduction wouldn't work on him. He rolled her over and came up on top, but when he tried to push up and away, she wrapped her legs around his waist, clutched his head and brought his mouth down to within a breath of those tantalizing mounds.

The sight of her creamy breasts sent his resolve scattering into the wind. He carefully cupped and eased them together then kissed each perfect bud. "I shouldn't be doing this."

"That's your frustration talking. But if you truly want to stop"—she lowered her legs to the sand and spread her arms out wide—"then go. I'd never force you to make love to me. Just know I'll keep your secret about your father and your birth. I would never judge you."

"You give so selflessly." Damn. Walking away from her would be impossible. She'd captivated him from the very beginning. What was one more night? He bent and devoured her breasts, licking and sucking each one in turn. "I wish I could be the man you need."

"Does this mean you're giving me a yes?" Arching into him, she stroked his scalp.

"Yes, until dawn, I'm all yours."

"Thank you." She unbuckled his belt, slid his zip down and freed him. "Because I want it hard and fast to start with. We could even call this make up sex. I've heard it's fantastic."

"It better not be." He didn't need the sex between them getting any hotter than it already was. He eased the hem of her dress up and rubbed his straining cock against her wet folds. "From now on, you never go out anywhere without any underwear on. That's an order."

"If you haven't noticed, I stopped taking your orders the second I boarded the ship." She cupped his butt and pulled him into her. "Make me scream, Hammers."

"We also need to talk about your desire to take control." He pushed in deeper, until her hot heat pulsed around him. Ahh, he loved the way she held onto him.

"That feels so good. Don't forget I want it hard." Panting, she rocked underneath him. "Like really hard. Move. Now. Make me come."

He claimed her lips and plundered her mouth while below, he plunged into her again and again.

"Oh, purrrfect." She pushed her hips forward, meeting every single one of his thrusts. His cock throbbed on the verge of release, and as she cried out, he bellowed and sank balls-deep inside her. He came, pulse after pulse jetting from him until every ounce of his energy was gone.

He tipped to his side, rolled and brought her up on top.

With their bodies still joined and limbs tangled, all he wanted to do was lie like this with her forever.

"Sooo good." Her eyelids fluttered shut and she sighed with

a wide smile. "Make up sex is everything I'd hoped for."

For him too, not that he'd ever tell her that. He closed his eyes. A few minutes' rest wouldn't hurt. Then he'd continue to love her throughout the remainder of the night.

He had until dawn, and he intended to make every moment count.

Chapter 5

The sun's dawn rays crept over Saria and warmed her, not that she wasn't already basking in the heat from Ben wrapped around her, and the sandy hollow they'd snuggled into a comfy cushion underneath. She opened her eyes to the new day and held perfectly still.

Ben's long golden lashes swept his cheeks, and his lips tugged upward as he slept. He'd made love to her twice more during the night, those times achingly slow and with complete devotion.

Gently, she kissed his closed eyelids, cheeks and nose. He stirred and his arms banded tighter around her. "You are courageous and determined, Ben Hammers. Never a burden, only a pillar of strength. My lover, and the only one I ever want to take."

He blinked, then flopped a hand over his eyes. "Ugh, too bright."

"Did you hear what I said?" She rose up onto one elbow so her shadow covered his face. "Look at me."

"I heard you." He lifted his hand and his blue gaze speared on hers. "I'll never want a wife, children, and all the trappings a family brings. We're the exact opposite. You love caring for others. For heaven's sakes, you're a trained nurse. You don't want to just care for those who you're closest to, but anyone and everyone in your vicinity."

"Wait up. I wasn't asking for all the trappings, but stating a fact. I simply wanted you to know how much I've loved spending this time with you. And you care for others as much as I do. Putting your life on the line counts, and far more than anything I've ever done does."

"As long as we understand each other." He hauled the neckline of her white dress up, gripped the trailing ties and made a bow around her neck. Smoothly, he eased her hemline down and brushed the sand from her arms and legs.

"I understand." No meant no, and he'd stated his preference loud and clear. "Thank you for the past day. It was incredibly special."

"For me too." He zipped his pants, straightened his shirt collar then pulled her to her feet. "Let's get back to the ship. You have a trip scheduled to the mainland today."

"And you're going fishing." She walked beside him along the shoreline. The frothy tipped waves rolled in and lapped her feet. The water both soothed and stung the odd scratch on her feet from her mad dash last night.

"Yeah, after I move my things into Brigs's cabin. I'll bunk down with him for the remainder of the trip." His blue shirttails flapped free in the fresh sea breeze. "You'll continue on with your life, and I'll do the same with mine."

"Ben, you've made your point loud and clear." Heart heavy, she trekked out of the surf toward the tree line where the resort lay not far beyond. Right now, she didn't care to hear how he wanted to distance himself from her. "I wanted to make an appointment with the doctor yesterday but got sidetracked. I should do that now. Could you let Lydia know I'm okay and I'll get back to the ship as soon as I can?"

"I'm not leaving you alone in the middle of the jungle." He lugged his cell phone from his pocket and made a call. "Tyler, it's Ben. We're on our way back, or we will be after a quick detour to the resort." His gruff voice rumbled over her from close behind as she walked. "What time's the flight?" A pause. "I'll have her back by then. Talk to you again soon."

Continuing on, she weaved through the trees.

"Tyler said the chopper leaves at nine sharp, and you and your sister have to check in every two hours." He passed her then lifted a low branch blocking her way.

"Thanks for calling him." She ducked underneath.

"Why the rush to see the doctor?"

"I need to get the hormone injection—ouch." She grabbed her foot. She'd stood right on top of a spiky twig poking through the bracken.

"Here, I'll carry you. I don't know how you ran through here last night and didn't get hurt." He tossed her over his shoulder and her belly thumped into his rock hard shoulder.

"Ben," she growled. "I'm sure there's a better way to carry me than this."

"Not when I need one hand free to move the branches." He patted her backside. "Or to ensure you don't slip out of my hold. You have the sweetest looking bottom by the way."

"Yours is pretty hot too." With a hand on each of his cheeks, she stroked his tight butt in slow circles. "More than hot."

"Stop it."

"You started it."

"I'm not in the right state of mind. You're without panties, and I haven't forgotten. Let's talk about something else." He kept one hand firm around the back of her knees as he walked. "After the wedding, what do you intend to do?"

"That would be sailing back to Auckland. Are you catching a flight or coming with us?"

"Catching a flight. Work calls. What about after you return home?"

"Do you mean where am I going to live?"

"Exactly."

"I've got a bit saved so I'll find somewhere to rent, and look at you getting all worried about me. You need to snap out of that." She gripped his back and eased herself up enough to loop her arms around his neck. The move made him lose his firefighter's hold, and she slid down his chest and into his arms. "That's better. A girl can get dizzy swinging around like that. Your penthouse apartment is right above your offices, isn't it?" He'd mentioned it a couple of times.

"Yeah."

"Your place must have a ton of space. Care for a roomie?"

"I live alone. Always have and always will."

"Mmm, yet you've been living with me for a year."

"There are times when I go where the jobs are, as in your case. We're here." He stepped out of the jungle and into the meadow. Sunshine bathed the tranquil spot. Gently, he set her on her feet.

"Thanks for the ride." She reached onto her toes and kissed his cheek. "And I mean every single one of them."

"Quit the sexy talk." He grabbed her hand and tugged her along the coral sandstone path toward the main four-story building. Others strolled along the nearby trails weaving in and around the thatch-roofed bures.

Inside the main building on the lower floor, the glass fronted pharmacy where she needed to make her appointment held a sign saying it opened at nine. She wandered to the clinic next door, tested the knob and found the door locked.

Ben tapped his thigh. "It opens right when you need to be winging your way to the mainland."

"Making an appointment will have to wait then. I'm not in a huge rush anyway, not since sex with you is off the cards." The delicious scents of cooked meats and tropical fruits floated to her on the breeze and distracted her. Her belly rumbled and she rubbed it. "Mmm, I might eat here rather than on the ship."

The open-air restaurant held a large servery in the center, while along the perimeter chefs attended four individual cooking stations.

"It's busy, Saria. Can you handle that kind of a crowd?"

"Hospitals hold crowds, and I need to get used to being around lots of people." She ran her fingers through her hair, tidying it as best as she could. Her dress wasn't too wrinkled, and Ben looked as gorgeous as ever, no matter how he was dressed. "Want to join me?"

"I'm not letting you eat alone." He set a hand at her lower back and guided her toward the short line of people waiting to be seated.

Two children bounced eagerly on their toes and tried to peer past their mother while their father stood next to them, a baby strapped in a capsule across his back. They were seated, and then the Polynesian woman wearing a yellow ankle-length island floral dress as all the waitresses did returned and welcomed them.

Ben's voice was firm as he asked for a table in the far corner where it appeared quietest. He gave his name and their ship's dock number for the bill as they took their seat.

Saria clutched her hands in her lap. This was far more crowded than the bridged walkway where she'd gotten jittery, but she wasn't boxed in here. She breathed slowly, rolled her shoulders and found her inner peace.

"We can take our time." Ben edged his chair closer to hers then tipped her chin up so she couldn't look anywhere but at him. His smile lit his blue eyes. "We'll go whenever you're ready and not before. Tell me what your favorite breakfast food is."

A wave of warmth crashed through her. He knew just how to divert her mind. She loved it when he fired questions at her. "Cheesy omelets. What's yours?"

"I'm extremely partial to your bacon and eggs. I love the

way you fry the bacon until it's perfectly crispy." He tucked a loose lock of her hair behind her ear. "My favorite dinner would be your spaghetti and meatballs."

"You always have so much fun eating that dish. I loved watching you wind the spaghetti on your fork and then try to get it into your mouth without dropping any. Almost every time you took a bite, you'd get sauce right here." She tapped his chin. "I always wanted to lick it off. I never said, but I did, so bad."

He groaned and fidgeted in his chair. "You're making me hard."

"I like—"

"Good morning, Saria."

"Oh, Dr. Hika. I didn't see you there."

In casual tan pants and a crisp white button-down shirt, he leaned a hand on the back of her chair. "I booked a seat this morning on the chopper and discovered I'm heading out with you and your sister shortly."

"That's fantastic. You'll get to meet Lydia." She motioned toward Ben. "This is Ben Hammers, my bodyguard extraordinaire."

"Nice to meet you, Ben. Saria mentioned you yesterday." He shook Ben's hand.

"It's nice to meet you too." Ben stretched, settled his arm across the back of her chair and curled his fingers around her nape. "I appreciate what you did for Saria, patching up her ankle."

"You're welcome, although it was all in the line of duty." He dipped his head toward her. "I'll let you two enjoy your breakfast. See you at nine."

"Yes, see you then." She patted Ben's upper leg. "I'm ready to eat if you are."

"I'm starving." He stood and offered her his hand. "Let's head to the chef preparing omelets first. One favorite breakfast coming up."

They weaved around the tables of chattering holidaymakers. At the cooking station, Ben planted her in front of him as he placed his order, his body a solid wall of warmth at her back. She loved how he made her feel so protected. She'd miss this, his continual presence. Unable to stop herself, she leaned back against him, relishing the moment.

"What would you like?" His breath tickled her cheek.

"A two-egg omelet with diced capsicum, tomato, and lots of cheese."

"Got it." He placed her order, and while their food was being prepared, led her to the central servery. With a plate in hand, he nodded toward the fresh fruit. "Stack it up, and add a handful of those nuts and raisins for extra energy."

"Good idea. I'll need a ton of that to keep up with Lydia. With the freedom she's about to experience, she'll be hard to pin down."

"You'll be careful, right? Follow all the regular safety rules." He tweaked her chin then frowned and slowly dropped his hand away. "Sorry, gotta stop touching you. Safety comes first, all right?"

"I won't forget, and we'll take good care of each other, as we always have." Whenever Ben had taken them shopping, for clothing or other personal necessities, he'd ushered them around in their disguises and made certain they were aware of any possible dangers. Even those times when she'd had to fulfill her practical hospital rotations, Ben had drilled into her what she had to watch out for. Most of those assignments though had been set within a secured ward, and he'd remained close by. She wouldn't have the safety blanket of having him on hand today, but everything he'd taught her was deeply ingrained and she'd never forget. "You have nothing to worry about."

"I'll worry nonetheless. It comes with the job."

She selected slices of pineapple, watermelon, and pawpaw for them both. With all he'd asked for plated up, she chose two glasses of freshly squeezed orange juice. "Lead the way to the table."

"Stay right behind me, one step, no more." Ben weaved ahead around the edge of the area and she followed through the throng. He hadn't needed to say such a thing. Old habits obviously died hard, for both of them.

At their table, she sat and popped a cube of sweet pineapple in her mouth. "Mmm, this is delicious."

"I'll go and grab our hot food. No moving from this area." He strode away to collect their order.

"Excuse me. Would you like a hot drink? Tea or coffee?" A dark-haired waitress held a teapot in one hand and a coffee pot in the other, her smile wide and welcoming.

"Two coffees please." No sudden jumping that time. She'd be able to tell Henry he could stop whistling when he drew near.

The woman poured steaming coffee into the two white cups sitting in the center of the table next to a dainty milk jug and sugar pot. After dipping her head, the waitress strolled on toward the next table.

"I watched. You did great." Ben set her plate in front of her, sat and picked up his knife and fork.

"I feel like a regular person. No more antagonizing fears for me." She ate and enjoyed every delicious mouthful of her omelet while he consumed his own. Finished, she added milk and sugar to their coffees and nudged Ben's cup toward him. "What will you tell Brigs and Tyler?"

"About…" He sipped his drink. "Ah, do you mean what I told you last night?"

"Yes. They'd both understand, and neither would pass judgment on you." They were best mates. He needed to open up to them, share some of his feelings.

"I'll think about it. Guys aren't the same as girls. We don't need to discuss every little thing. We have boundaries we don't cross."

"That's silly. Boundaries are meant to be crossed, and discussion is good for the soul. Where are your parents these days?" The subject would be a touchy one, but unless she kept pushing him to talk, he'd never open up on his own. She squeezed his hand. "Tell me."

"The man who fathered me passed away while serving time for the double rape. I never met him, just received the notification through the system he'd died of a heart attack. Mary Hammers lives in England. Three months after I was born, she left the country and never returned."

The pain of his mother's abandonment had to have hurt, no matter the reason. She cupped his cheek. "You were an innocent child, and if I have to tell you that a million times, I will."

"And you deserve the very best. One day you'll find the right man." He gulped his coffee down and scraped his chair back. "Come on. Time's marching on. You can't miss your flight."

Their conversation wasn't finished, but she did need to leave.

* * * *

In her room, she changed into a long, cap-sleeved cream dress with a lacy yellow waist panel while he dressed in black chinos and a dark blue cotton t-shirt.

She snuck into the bathroom, combed her hair and brushed her teeth as Ben edged in behind her, collected his toiletries from the vanity drawer then returned to the bedroom. She trailed him, then propped one hip against the bathroom doorjamb. She'd hate not being able to see him first thing in the morning like this after sleeping beside him for two long months. Even now, every inch of her ached to go to him. "I'll miss you."

"I'll only be down the passageway." With a determined hand, he shoved the rest of his belongings into his duffel and slung it over his shoulder. Gaze on hers, he drummed his fingers on his leg. "Do you have your cell phone?"

"Yes, but it'll be flat by now." It still sat on the coffee table in front of the couch where she'd last left it. She picked it up and popped it onto the charger. "Lydia will have hers."

"You have to call. Every two hours, okay?" He dragged her to him, tucked her head under his chin and held her. A long goodbye hug, and not nearly what she wanted. Gently, he pulled away. "Travel safely."

"Sure. Enjoy Brigs's spare bunk."

"I will," he grumbled and shut the door behind him.

Gone. Her heart heaved. The one man she wanted was the only one she could never have.

* * * *

Ben tossed his bag onto the top bed in Brigs's cabin. It was a small, efficient space with two bunks bolted to a blue painted wall. White furnishings and a built-in set of drawers completed the room. "You there, Brigs?"

"Yo." Brushing his teeth, he opened the bathroom door. "Did you get tossed out of Saria's room already?"

"No, I bailed." He squeezed past Brigs and slid his toiletries into the second drawer. The compact area included a shower cubicle, toilet and vanity, all in basic white. No frills like Saria's stateroom, but he didn't need any. "I'm ready to haul in a prize catch."

"Are you talking about a fish or some other kind of catch?"

"A damn fish." He stalked back into the cabin and plunked into the corner wicker chair.

"What's put you in such a foul mood?" Wiping his face with a washcloth, Brigs followed him. "You wanna talk about it?"

"No. Yes. I opened up to Saria last night." He slumped forward, elbows on his knees. "About my childhood."

"You? Opened up? I don't believe it." Brigs let out a low whistle. "You know you can always talk to me too. I have sisters. I'm used to the whole 'gotta talk things out stuff' that chicks dig."

"I'm not a chick." Still, Brigs and Tyler were his right hand men. The three of them had been together for more years and untold scrapes than he could count. Saria hadn't condemned him for the details surrounding his unfortunate birth, and maybe both his best mates wouldn't either. "My father was one of the dirtiest scumbags on the planet." The words tumbled from him. No holding back now. "At forty-five, he got out of jail after serving time for one count of rape, only to turn around two days later and rape two eighteen-year-old women. One was to be my mother."

"Serious?" He blew out a long breath. "I'm so sorry."

"He was convicted and imprisoned again. Then not long before I left the foster system, I received word he'd died."

"What about your mother? Is she still alive?"

"She gave me up and never looked back. I had her searched though and sometimes check in on what she's up to. She has a husband and a couple of teenagers. They seem to be doing all right, all four of them."

"So you've never made contact?"

"No, and I never will. A nice woman like that doesn't need her past coming back to haunt her."

"That explains a lot, why you're as dedicated to protecting others as you are. You had no one to protect you as a kid."

"What?" He'd never let Brigs get away with glorifying his job like that. "So, you're not fazed by my past at all?"

"No, but you clearly are. You've got to let it go, Ben."

"Telling you is a step in the right direction." Saria was right, and telling Brigs had helped. Except now he needed to tell Tyler the truth.

He scrubbed his face then groaned as overhead, the whop-whop of the chopper's blades buzzed then faded out toward sea. That aircraft held the one person he wanted to keep at his side, and every instinct urged him to fight for her, to get her back and plead for her to give him some time to work through his issues.

If only life really worked that way. Sure, she'd accepted his past, but that didn't change the fact his future was set in stone. No commitment. No relationships. He was a loner, and always would be.

"She'd be good for you." Brigs opened the door and jerked his head toward the passageway. "If you let Saria get away, I'm certain you'll come to regret it."

"She might be good for me, but I've got too much baggage for it to ever work." He stomped past Brigs and down the corridor.

"Nothing she couldn't handle though. She's a tough cookie."

"Give it up, Brigs." He jogged upstairs and onto the deck. "We've a job to do. Best we both focus on that."

"Are you calling me a job?" Tyler, leaning against the stern rail, eyed them as they approached.

"Never." Ben clapped him on the back. "It's distraction time. Show me the fish."

Chapter 6

With the sky and ocean an endless shade of blue along the horizon, Saria's flight to Nadi should have been awe-inspiring. Instead, every mile away from Ben had her heart aching, harder and heavier. It wasn't right, leaving him when they still had so much to talk about.

"You okay, sis?" Lydia nudged her arm. "We're almost at the mainland and you haven't said a word the entire trip."

"Sorry, I don't mean to be bad company."

In the seat opposite them, Dr. Hika stopped rummaging through his briefcase and glanced at her. "You do look pale. Is there anything I can do to help?"

"If you can fix my bodyguard that'd be great."

"You can speak freely to me whenever you'd like to, and so can Ben. I minored in psychology, and I love a good sit-down session. I also have my mother's nosy-nose." He tapped said nose.

She smiled. "I'd love an outsider's perspective on my situation, but I'm afraid I can't go into the details of Ben's difficult childhood, not when he told me in confidence."

"I understand, and it's not easy when we can see someone else needs help and they don't." He locked his briefcase and set it by his feet. "Maybe in time he will, or if he's given a little push. What of yourself?"

"My world is changing. I need to start looking for a job and a place to live." She also wanted to be there for the one man who needed her. If only he'd let her.

"Yes, you're a nurse." A glitter lit his eyes. "And if you're truly after a job, maybe I can help. I have a proposition for you."

"I love propositions. Fire away." This certainly sounded intriguing, and she needed the distraction.

"Another reason I'm heading to the mainland, other than to collect some necessary supplies, is to search for a new nurse for the island. With over three-thousand tourists at any one time, I require additional aid."

"What happened to your nurse?"

"She was called away a week ago. A family emergency. Which means I need to temporarily fill the position until she returns. About another four weeks."

Excitement thrummed through her. This could be exactly what she needed, even though it meant a short time away from Lydia. Oh, and the islands. A magical place to work, even if only for a month. Her spirits lifted. "Tell me more."

"The position comes with free accommodation at the resort as well as meals and laundry. The hours are nine to five weekdays, but you'd need to remain on-call at night and on weekends, the same as I do."

"Keep going." This was a dream come true.

"The patients I see are generally relaxed, and their ailments minor. If anyone requires surgery, they're flown to the mainland, so your duties would be more similar to those required in a general practitioner's office."

"I can't believe you're offering me a job and a place to live." She jiggled in her seat. "You're not worried about my recent fears?"

"As far as I can see, there're almost nonexistent. Certainly if you experience any problems, I'll be right on hand. It's also very rare for me to have a runaway cleaner's trolley or a stampeding crowd in the office." He grinned. "Would you consider the position?"

"I'd love to consider it." She clasped Lydia's hand. "Do you have any problem with me saying yes?"

"I think it sounds perfect, and I'll only be a phone call away." Lydia hugged her. "We're not running or in hiding anymore. It's time for us to live again."

"Then that's what I'll do." She extended her hand to the doctor. "You've got yourself a new nurse. When would you like me to start?"

* * * *

The wooden dinghy rocked as Ben leaned over the side and tossed his line. So far, he'd caught three massive sea slugs, a starfish and more seaweed than could possibly be floating at the bottom of all that crystalline blue. His level of frustration at having Saria so far from him had also escalated to the point where he was ready to blow.

Brigs wasn't helping any either lying sprawled asleep across the center seat. Ben lifted his foot and tapped Brigs's dangling leg. With his cap pulled low over his face and his springy black hair poking out from underneath, Brigs snorted but didn't wake. How could the man snooze when the girls weren't here?

"We should toss him overboard." Tyler held his rod in one hand and his cell phone in the other. He stared at the device then gave it a shake as if that would make it miraculously ring.

Ben wanted to shake the phone as well. "When Lydia calls, I want to speak to Saria, and I won't accept any more of her excuses about saying she can't talk to me." Every time Lydia had rung, she'd told him Saria was busy trying on one dress or another, and as yet he hadn't spoken to her. It was almost four in the afternoon, seven horrendously long hours since she'd flown out.

"It's crappy not being in control, right?" Tyler blew out a

long breath.

"From now on, you don't agree to any shopping excursions for those girls without my direct authorization."

"I didn't exactly agree. This was Lydia's idea."

"You agreed when you didn't disagree." The girls were both on their own. Without a guard. Ben should've ignored their request to go it alone and hopped on board the chopper with them. "I'm going to go crazy if I don't hear from Saria soon."

"I'll make sure Lydia puts her on." Tyler shoved a hand through his hair. "Hell, even your news this morning about your sleaze of a father didn't manage to distract me nearly long enough." Tyler hadn't condemned him either, not even for all the years he'd withheld the information. "Maybe you shouldn't have ended things yet with Saria." Tyler fiddled with his rod. "You're clearly uncomfortable letting her go."

"It would never work."

"Did Saria say that?"

"No, I said that. Sleepyhead there"—he jabbed a finger at Brigs—"tried to convince me letting her go would be wrong too, but that's what I've done, and I'm sticking to that decision." He held out his hand. "Pass me that damn phone. I've had enough of waiting."

Tyler handed it over and Ben punched in Lydia's number.

"Hello, honey." Lydia's voice, as sweet as sugar, resonated down the line. "I still had one more minute before I had to call you."

"It's not your honey. It's Ben. Put Saria on, and I don't want to hear any more excuses. Not one."

"I can't put her on. She's filling in paperwork for her new job."

"What?" He tapped the phone. "This connection must be acting up. Did you say paperwork for a new job?"

"Yes, she got the offer this morning, but told me not to say anything until the deal was all signed and sealed. We're at the hospital now with Dr. Hika. He wanted everything recorded formally. You know, so she's covered for any eventuality, insurance and all. We've already organized a Fijian bank account for her wages."

"What job are you talking about? Saria doesn't have a job." She couldn't work here, not when she'd be too far away from him. His heart started beating out of time.

"She accepted a nursing position with Dr. Hika. She'll be staying on at Resort Island once we've sailed away."

"For how long?" He thumped his chest, got his ticker back onto the right beat.

"Only four weeks. The nurse who usually holds the position is dealing with a family illness. I'm so excited for—oh, here she is. You can talk to her now. Saria, Ben's on the phone. He wants to talk to you." A crackle came down the line then all went quiet. Lydia must have covered the mouthpiece.

He rapped one foot on the dinghy's floorboards where a little water sloshed within the hull.

"What's happening?" Tyler leaned forward, his gaze narrowed.

"Saria's accepted a job as a nurse here at the island. A temporary one, but I don't like it."

"Ben, she's too busy to talk to you right now." Lydia was back. "Sorry, but we've got to catch a cab and get back to the helipad. Tell Tyler I love him. See you guys soon." She hung up and a piercing tone buzzed in his ear.

Lydia had not just hung up on him. And Saria had certainly never been too busy to speak to him whenever he'd called. What the hell was going on?

"Well, what did Lydia say?" Tyler held out his hand for the phone and he passed it back.

"They're catching a cab now to the helipad, and she said she loves you." He scrubbed his face with numb fingers. "Saria can't take a job here."

"Why not?"

"Because I can't reach her quick enough if she needs me." He hauled his line in, including another bunch of useless seaweed he wanted to toss at snoring Brigs.

"Hey." Tyler gripped his shoulder. "Calm down. She's no longer in The Program. She shouldn't have a need for you to get to her."

Tyler was right, only Ben couldn't stand he was.

They weren't in a relationship, and never would be. That hurt almost as much as the thought of her being so far away.

* * * *

Saria jiggled in her seat as the chopper flew in over the island then settled with a gentle bump on the resort's concrete landing pad. The blades whirred down and Lydia squeezed past her and bounded out. Tyler waited by the storage shed to the side of the tennis courts in tan shorts and a brown and white striped t-shirt. Lydia ran into Tyler's arms and he swung her about, sending her knee-length lilac skirt flying. She adored how much Tyler loved her sister.

"I'll get your purchases for you." Dr. Hika hopped out then grasped the large box holding Lydia's wedding gown and her bridesmaid dress. The shop assistant had carefully wrapped both in white tissue paper after they'd made their final selection.

"Thanks." She climbed out onto the helipad after him. Her hair whipped around her face and she tucked it behind her ears.

The sun was close to setting, and the last couple who'd been playing tennis closed the wire gate and handed their rackets and balls to the attendant standing inside the beachside bright yellow sports kiosk.

Dr. Hika handed her the box then reached back in for his briefcase. "If you're still after that appointment, instead of trying to make one at the pharmacy, I could see you during my lunch break tomorrow."

"You don't mind?"

"Certainly not. You can take a look through the nurse's office and get comfortable with where everything is."

"That'd be perfect." She didn't start until Monday, once the others had sailed.

"See you tomorrow afternoon at one." He waved and strolled away.

Tyler strode across, took the box from her and grinned. "Thanks for keeping an eye on your sister for me."

"Anytime, although it was more the other way around today. She found her dress straight away, while I took forever." She slung her purse over her shoulder and followed him and Lydia along the wharf as they nattered.

They boarded, and she hurried down the stairwell. Guilt still ate at her for not taking Ben's call earlier, but she wasn't ready to talk to him about her decision to take the job and remain here.

She snuck into her room, locked the door and leaned her forehead against it.

"About time you got back."

She spun about, banging her hip on the brass doorknob. "Ben, what are you doing here?"

"We need to talk." He rose from the white leather couch and stared her down.

"I—I—" Her gut clenched.

He raised one blond eyebrow in a hard angle. "Did you have a nice day on the mainland?"

"Yes. What about you? Catch any fish?"

"Not one."

"That's a shame." Now he was in her room, he'd demand an answer. She nibbled on her bottom lip. There must be some way she could sidetrack him. "I bought a new dress and some shoes as well."

"I'm more interested in this new job you've got." He pressed her against the door, his chest rising and falling heavily. "Explain yourself."

She was out of time. "I was presented with an opportunity I couldn't turn down, and it's only temporary."

"I'm aware it's temporary." He slid his fingers in under her hair and around the nape of her neck. With his other hand, he played with the top button of her dress. "For an entire four weeks."

"What are you doing?" She desperately wanted him to undo that button, and the next.

"Nothing." He held her, his rapid heartbeat pounding against hers. "I'm doing absolutely nothing, as agreed."

She wrapped her arms around his waist and held on.

In the quiet, the day's frustrations melted away, and a sense of rightness stole over her. The setting sun sent a blaze of gold shimmering across the walls.

"I told Brigs and Tyler everything." His words rumbled over her.

"Did they take it well?" She hid her smile in his shirtfront.

"Yes, and I should have told them years ago. I know you're smiling and thinking I-told-you-so."

"I'd never do any such thing. I'm enjoying the moment." She rubbed her cheek against his chest. "Is there anything else you want to tell me since we're having this heart to heart?"

"I've never known what it's like to have a true home."

"Keep going." Her heart lifted. Finally, he was opening up.

"The first time I ever had a room to myself was after I left the army and started up my own firm."

"How did that happen? What made you set out on your own?"

"It's not a secret. One of the men in my dorm room heard about an outside job going over the Christmas holidays. A bodyguard was needed and the pay was good. Since I was due some leave, I offered to take it. It wasn't like I had anywhere else to go during the holidays. No family and all."

"No, but you have wonderful friends." She looped one

finger through his belt hoop. "Who was the job for?"

"A wealthy actor. The studio he worked for took me on to do another job following that one. In the end, I had to keep extending my leave to cover the additional work. Three months all up."

"You enjoyed the work?"

"Yes. Referral after referral came in, and before I knew it, I could no longer handle the number of assignments on my own. I left the army for good, and at that point, Brigs and Tyler joined me. Within two years, I had more than a dozen men on staff. I expanded, rented a city office, and from there began accepting local authority and government contracts. I've never looked back."

"I'm glad it was you who took on my job."

"When your report came across my desk and I discovered two innocent women were running for their lives, I couldn't turn either of you down. Two sisters within one family. Hell, had your parents or brothers lost you, I would never have lived with myself. They're good folks."

Ben met with her parents occasionally, gave them updates and assured them he'd see their case solved and their daughters returned to them. It meant the world to her that he did. And when a secured line could be patched through to her family, she and Lydia got to speak to them.

"You have the biggest heart." She looked into his eyes, and a touch of the rising moonlight tracking through lit the sky-blue depths and made her pulse race. "I'm so lucky to have you."

"It's the other way around." He twined a lock of her hair around his finger. "It's almost dinner time. Would you like me to escort you upstairs?"

"No, I'm going to take a shower first. You may escort me there if you wish."

"Don't tempt me." He twirled her away from the door then opened it. With one last look over his shoulder, he blew her a kiss then left her alone in the dark.

"Scaredy-cat," she called through the closed door.

His chuckle echoed down the passageway.

85

Chapter 7

Impatient, Ben paced the pristine white carpet of the clinic's waiting room as Saria had her doctor's appointment the next afternoon. The empty nurse's area, located behind a high wooden curved front desk was where she'd be working come Monday morning. Without him.

Hell, he was leaving her all alone, in the middle of the South Pacific without even any family. What kind of a man did that?

He should stay. It would be easy enough to ask his office assistant to organize one of his bodyguards to cover for him with the next job. He shoved his hand through his hair and raked his fingers across his scalp. Except Saria would be safe here. Her desk was right next to the doctor's office. Still, he couldn't shake these nerves.

At the window, he gripped the polished wooden sill. Outside, the resort's lush gardens and countless coconut trees swished in the breeze. Not even the amazing view could relax him.

The office door opened and Saria walked out, her long luscious brown locks swaying. Rosy-cheeked, she smiled at him. "Dr. Hika's free for another twenty minutes if you'd like to see him."

"Thanks." He'd asked her to check if he could have some

time. He needed to make certain the doctor understood all her needs. "Where will you be?"

"Right here. I need to get acquainted with this area and ensure I know where everything is stored."

"Good. Remain here, and don't move from this spot." He caught her chin, desperately wanting to plant a kiss on her lips. Sleeping apart from her last night had been hell, and when he'd finally napped, his dreams had revolved around her.

"Relax. I'll be right here." She sashayed toward the cupboards, popped her bottom out as she bent then gave it a wiggle. Her pink skirt's short ruffled layers beckoned him to flip them then smooth his hands down her creamy legs and touch every inch of her body. She better damn well be wearing panties today.

"Do you have a uniform?"

"When I was in Nadi, I was issued with my work whites." She peered into the cupboards and moved things about. "Stop procrastinating and go and see the doctor."

"Sure, but I won't be long." He dragged himself away from her, knocked on the door she'd left open and nodded at the doctor. "Is it all right to come in?"

"Yes, take a seat, Ben. Make yourself comfortable." He closed a file with Saria's name emblazoned across the top then slotted it into place on a corner carousel filled with similar manila folders. "Anywhere you like."

Two gray padded chairs sat in front of the doctor's solid walnut desk, but instead of choosing one of those, he wandered around the coffee table and settled on the long forest green couch nestled under the window. "Nice office."

"Thanks. Sometimes I end up sleeping in here on long nights, and the couch makes a good bed." He picked up a pen and pad from the corner of his desk and sank into the swivel chair opposite him. The black leather creaked as it welcomed his weight. "What did you want to chat about?"

"Saria."

"Right." He tapped the pad. "I'll answer what I can, provided it doesn't overstep the boundaries of patient or employee confidentiality."

"You don't need to answer anything, just listen." From his wallet, he handed over a business card. "My contact details. Should she need anything, for any reason, call me. Her safety and wellbeing are my responsibility."

"She said before you came in here, you might do this." He slipped a card from his shirt pocket and waved it. "I already have one of your cards, compliments of Saria."

"Take both. You can keep one in your office, and one on you."

"Well, thank you." Smiling, he slotted the card back in his top pocket. "Most appreciated, although you should have more confidence in Saria's ability to look after herself."

"I have the utmost confidence in her ability." He certainly wouldn't be leaving her here if that weren't the case.

"Good." The doctor eased back and crossed one leg over his knee. "So, we've time to kill. You can speak freely if you wish. Certainly anything you say will remain between us."

"Saria's my life." The words shot from his mouth before he could register them. "I mean, she's important to me. I can't have any harm coming to her."

"I'll look after her. You have my word on that."

"This past year, we've gotten close." He'd bottled things up for so long, that his thoughts had nowhere to go but out.

"She mentioned that, and although no details were discussed, she did say you'd had a difficult childhood."

"More like a nonexistent one. My father was the worst kind of criminal, and my mother an innocent. I was the result. All I can say is the past is the past."

"Yes, unless of course our past affects our future." His focused gaze became more intent. "If you don't mind me asking, where do you see yourself in say five years, or even ten?"

"I'll still be doing what I love. Protecting others."

"An admirable job, and what about Saria? Where do you see her in that same length of time?"

"With a man who can give her what she needs and children running around her feet." His heart wrenched at the thought, that she'd accept another man into her life.

"For that to happen, you'd have to let her go. Is that something you want to do?"

"No." He couldn't break all ties with her. The only light in his life would be gone, forever.

"What are you thinking right now?" The doctor edged forward with a squeak of his chair's wheels. "Open up, Ben. Give yourself the freedom to speak and know someone wishes to listen and understand. Like you, all I desire is to help others."

"I have nothing to offer her. I don't want a family."

"Is there a particular reason why not?"

"All my life, I've lived with the stigma of how I came into this world. My birth should never have been, and wouldn't have except for one man deciding he could take it all. I won't follow in his path. His line ends with me."

"So, you're punishing yourself for your father's misdeeds?"

"Not punishing, ensuring order is restored, and no else can do that but me."

"I see, but there appears to be one flaw in your argument." The doctor slowly breathed out. "In the process of ensuring this order, what if you're also punishing Saria, the woman you've chosen to protect?"

"I'm not. I'm giving her the freedom she deserves."

"Is that how she sees it too?"

"I'm not sure."

"Then I hope you'll consider asking her." He walked around his desk, foraged in a drawer and returned with a card. "For you. These are my contact details, and should you ever need anything, for any reason, then call me. The safety and wellbeing of every patient who walks through my door is my responsibility.”

“You’re good, Doc, very good. You should be a shrink.” He pocketed it, stood and extended his hand. “Thanks for the conversation.”

“You’re welcome, and anytime.”

He left the doctor, closed the door then perched on the corner of Saria’s new desk.

Reading papers in a folder, she stood before a three-drawer metal filing cabinet, her studious frown so endearing.

“Do you think I’m punishing you, Saria?”

“Punishing me for what?” She slid the folder away and closed the drawer.

“For saying no to a relationship with you.”

“We both agreed there’d be no commitment and I can handle that, but do you think you’re punishing me?” She walked toward him, wrapped her arms around his neck and hugged him. “Or is it more important for you to right the wrongs of your past, which I might add, were never your fault in the first place.”

“Clearly you and the doctor have an understanding. You speak the same language.”

“No, I only have an understanding with you, and yes, I’d like more, but I’d never ask you for it. Not when I know you’d turn me down.”

“Is that how you truly feel?”

“Yes, but I’m not condemning you for that decision.” She breathed warm air against his neck as she popped a kiss there. “I’m just stating the facts. After my sister gets married, you’re leaving. You’ve made your position very clear.”

“So where do we go from here?”

“You hold all the cards, so we go nowhere.” She stepped back, picked up her purse, and strode out of the room.

“Hey, where are you going? We haven’t finished talking.”

"To check out my new room. Dr. Hika gave me the key code."

He followed her. Inspecting where she'd soon be living was high on his list of priorities. He needed to ensure the area was completely secure.

* * * *

Saria walked upstairs to room 410, punched the code into the lock then stepped inside. Sunshine streamed into the room through the sheer white nets and played its lacy pattern over the cream and gold striped wallpaper. The open window next to the ranch slider blew the nets inward and circulated the sweet aroma from the pink bougainvillea trailing along the deck's handrail. She crossed to the bed, sat and patted the brown and golden leafed bedcovers. "This is nice. What'd ya think?"

"The bed looks comfy." Ben shoved one hand in the pocket of his black denim shorts as he strolled around the room. "The window is security latched. You'll be able to leave it open as you please."

"What about the balcony? Can trespassers get in?"

He stepped outside, peered over the balustrade then returned. "It's all good. No one can swing in here uninvited. Thanks for giving the doctor my card by the way. Did you sort out what you needed to with him?"

"I tried. I wanted to get another injection. You have to have them every three months to maintain protection." She really didn't want to have to explain all this girl stuff to him, but he deserved to know what she'd found out. "Apparently my timing is a little out, but not by much. Now I have to wait until my next cycle starts before I can get it done."

"Which means what?" He paled.

"Nothing major." She poked her head into the bathroom. Lovely soothing colors of peach and cream greeted her, as well as a massive mirror along one wall, which reflected the bedroom and Ben towering behind her. "The chances of me falling pregnant are incredibly slim. The protection I was on usually has an overlapping period of a week or so, and it's not like we're doing it anymore. I simply should've had the shot before I sailed. That's all."

"You're sure it's nothing?"

"Absolutely."

"Then let's get some fresh air and take a walk." He tugged her out the door, jabbed the elevator button then steered her inside. From the v-neckline of his black shirt, he swiped his sunglasses hanging over one edge and slid them on.

"Where are we going for this walk?"

"The beach," he answered.

"Great. I have my bikini on underneath. I'd love a swim." The elevator doors opened onto the ground floor and she raced ahead. Instead of taking the main entrance, she snuck out the side door leading to the meadow, which would bypass the crowds.

"The jungle is this way, not the beach." Ben marched behind her.

"Dr. Hika and I walked out here the other day. Luke turned up and showed me a small gap in the trees. There's a path to the beach, but it's a tight fit."

"I'd rather do something which doesn't require me watching you strip down to two flimsy pieces of material. Bikinis should be outlawed, particularly on you."

"You've seen me in less. I think you can handle a little of my bare skin." She shuffled through the thin gap between the bushes and down onto the beach. "It's less populated here too."

"You go for a swim, and I'll"—his cell phone beeped and he pulled it out of his pocket—"answer this." He turned away. "Hammers. Yeah, I'm still in the islands with the girls. What's up, Gilchrist?"

She lifted her cream tank top over her head, tossed it onto the sand then tightened the top ties of her bikini. Four or five hundred feet offshore, waves broke over a short coral reef. Two men sitting at the stern of a small boat tanked up then flipped off the back end and disappeared under the water. She had to go diving along this reef while she was here. It would be so much fun. She shimmied out of her pink skirt, dropped it on top of her shirt then walked into the gloriously warm water.

Ben paced the beach as he continued his conversation with Gilchrist. She waved and he groaned. So stubborn. Sure, they weren't well-matched when it came to what they wanted in life, but in every other way, they were. If only he'd take a chance with her.

She walked in then at waist-depth, dived. Stunning blue starfish graced the sandy bottom while multicolored tropical fish darted around and snuck close as if hoping for a feed. Next time she came swimming, she'd bring some bread or fish food.

After coming up for air, she dove again then kicked out toward the reef. A swish of sand plumed on the base as a stingray far below shot off. It glided along to a clear spot and settled again. The ocean was alive and so beautiful. She swam to the surface and floated on her back.

On the beach, Ben stripped off his black shirt, rolled his cell phone into the folds then tucked it beside her clothes. The sunshine bathed his chest and tanned pecs. Then he slid his denim shorts down and exposed slim black swim trunks. It looked like he'd changed his mind and decided to come swimming with her after all. Nice.

He ran into the water then swam out toward her, his strokes powerful and fluid. With a splash, he stopped and treaded water. "I didn't think you'd head this far out."

"There's a coral reef on this side of the island, so we're fairly protected."

"Sharks can still swim in over by the wharf. If The Idle Dream can sail in, so can the dangerous marine life."

"What are you trying to say?" She drifted closer toward him

on her back. "That I'd make a tasty meal?"

"You'd be a treat no shark could turn down." He swept his hand under her back and tugged her up against him. His gaze remained glued to hers, so heart-pounding precious. "Your eyes are the richest, darkest shade of brown. I love it when you look at me."

"And yours are the same pale blue as the sky, the most soothing color I've ever seen."

"I hate my eyes. They're the same as my father's. I even have his blond hair."

"No, don't go there. You're nothing like him, even if you share some of the same physical characteristics." She wrapped her arms around his neck and he took her full weight in the water. "Lydia and I are identical and share all of the same physical attributes. Have you ever felt she's me?"

"Hell, no. She's nothing like you." His gaze narrowed and he snorted. "I can see where you're heading with this."

"You weren't even raised by him, yet emotionally he's had a huge influence over you. It's time for you to let that go. Stop allowing a dead man to dictate what you can and can't do, now and in the future."

"I made a vow to remain alone and I intend to honor it."

"I love that you honor your vows, but I'd rather you be more selective in the ones you make. Being alone surely isn't as much fun as spending time with those you're closest to." She played her fingers through his wet locks. "Make another vow to me. I want to strike a new deal. Let's extend our time together. Wouldn't you like a little more fun?"

"No." He smoothed over her bottom and brought her up against his hard shaft. "Feel that? I'm more like my father than you can imagine. I want to take you right here, right now, even though there are people just along the beach."

"Then we've got a problem, because I want that too." She stroked his broad shoulders. "Does that make me like your father as well?"

"You wouldn't even have considered what I said until I mentioned it."

"Maybe, but my thoughts were heading in that direction. Trust me. I wouldn't have been far behind." She traced along his lower lip. "I've missed your mouth on mine, and I'm desperate for it back."

"Saria." He jerked away and dropped her.

She sank under the water and came back up spluttering. She shoved her hair out of her face and splashed him. "That wasn't funny."

"You needed a cool off, and after the call I just took from Agent Gilchrist, I really should be focused on getting you back to the ship and ensuring your safety. Let's go. I'll explain the call once we're there." He stroked slowly toward the shore, making certain she was close.

The only kind of call that would cause him to worry would be if it related to hers and Lydia's case. Except their case was solved. Gilchrist had charged all those involved and ensured they were behind bars. At hip-depth, she stood and waded out. She flapped the sand from her skirt and wriggled it on over her damp skin "Tell me about the call."

"It's not news I expected to hear." He hauled his clothes on, slid his sunglasses into his top pocket then picked up her cream tank top and held it out. "Arms up."

"What's got you so worried?" She lifted her hands.

He slipped her shirt over her head and tugged it down. "Mia Taita's high-powered lawyer has managed to get her out of jail. There should have been enough evidence to hold her until Gilchrist could form a more solid case, but apparently not." He steered her along the beach toward the wharf, his shoes and her sandals swinging in his hand.

Oh, not good. Mia Taita's brother had been killed in a hit-and-run, and Lydia had witnessed it. The woman was the sole heir to Taita Software, one of the nation's most lucrative businesses, and speculation was Mia had contracted the killer to take her brother out. "What's Gilchrist going to do?"

"He's not going to rest until he gets Mia Taita back behind bars. She's the instigator, even though it was Kern Hyena who did the job. We just need more than the current circumstantial evidence to get a full conviction." A seagull squawked and took flight from the wharf's corner post as they stepped past it. "Gilchrist and his team are back on the case. They intend to pin her down, and fast."

"The Hyena brothers are still behind bars, right?"

"Yes, neither Kern nor Ladd can get to either of you. The case against them is solid, just not the woman who sent them." Ben guided her onto the ship and through the lounge toward the ship's private office on the second floor. "Her being out is risky, Saria. We'll need to take all the necessary precautions to ensure neither of you falls prey to her again. Anything is possible."

"We're not going under again are we?" They couldn't. They were just getting their lives back on track.

"Gilchrist wants his star witness kept safe."

"Which is Lydia, not me."

"What happens to one of you happens to both of you. You know that." He closed the office door behind them. Ben nodded her toward the blue and beige pinstriped couch. She sat and gripped the edge under her knees. "I asked Gilchrist to call Tyler and Brigs with the news. They should be here soon."

"Lydia's going to be peeved. She's so tired of running." Sunlight streamed through the partially turned cream blinds and lit stripes across the white shag carpet and huge mahogany desk holding a laptop that looked very familiar. The yellow sticker on the top held Ben's name. "You brought your laptop on holiday?"

"I never go anywhere without it, same as my weapons." He sat behind the desk, lifted the lid and turned it on. "I'm going to try to close your new Fijian bank account. Knowing Mia Taita, she'll find that with ease. Give me the bank number."

She rattled it off and he typed it in. "If you cancel Lydia's request for a marriage license, she'll kill you."

"She doesn't have a choice. I need all documentation leading to you two being on or near this island extinguished. We're dealing with a woman who's a computer genius and has a habit of getting the information she needs. I'll also chat to the local authorities, let them know of the possible problem." He slid out of the chair and before the corner safe, knelt and keyed in an unlock sequence. He removed a gun, checked the safety then slotted it into the back rise of his shorts.

"Saria." Lydia raced into the room in a short yellow sundress and floppy hat, Tyler and Brigs hot on her heels. "Did you hear? Mia Taita's out of jail."

"I heard. I'm sorry this has happened right before your wedding." Non-wedding now. She hugged her sister, squeezing her extra hard.

"We can deal with it, as long as we're together."

Tyler fetched his weapon from the safe. "We need to ship out, immediately."

"Got anywhere specific in mind?" Brigs asked as he buckled his holster on and slid his gun into place.

"I know the perfect spot." Tyler nodded and eyed Ben. "There's a secluded cove around the other side of this island. There's no way for anyone to get there except through the jungle, and the central mountainous plateau isn't all that easy to cross. It's where I hid Lydia before Gilchrist turned up and took her through re-identification. It's completely safe, yet if the girls wish, they can enjoy the private beach and not feel caged in, that's after we get it fully secured."

"Sounds good to me." Ben returned to his laptop. "It's best we remain somewhere close by anyway. We need to be able to pick up the island's exceptional phone and data coverage so we can stay in touch with the team back home. The satellite link isn't always that reliable as I've come to learn, and we certainly can't miss any of their communications. I'll forward our new location to Gilchrist."

"And I'll go and find my brothers and get them back on board." Tyler wrapped an arm around Lydia's waist and popped a kiss on her forehead. "This means our wedding has to go on hold."

"Why am I not surprised?" She shook her head despondently.

"I'll take you to our room." Tyler walked her out the door.

Saria edged around the desk and faced Ben. "I think you've forgotten I have work on Monday."

He eyed Brigs. "Could you deal with that before we leave? Speak to the good doctor and inform him he's lost his nurse. Let him know she's had to return to protective custody. Also, have him remove all record of her coming employment. Not a trace can be left of the girls' arrival or stay here. You can trust him with whatever information you need to ensure his compliance. I talked to him earlier. He's trustworthy."

"No problem. I'm onto it." Brigs left and shut the door behind him.

"Come here." Ben pulled her down onto his lap then continued typing with his arms around her.

She rubbed his chest through his damp shirt. "Are you all right?"

"I will be once Mia Taita is locked away. She's the one loose end I can't stand."

"Me too." She breathed deep, slowly in and out, although no panic rose. Lydia was safe in her room and Ben was safe right here.

They'd beat this, as long as they all stayed together.

Chapter 8

Ben swept Saria's silky brown hair over her shoulder as she nestled against his chest at the office desk. She'd fallen asleep and not wanting to wake her, he'd continued with his work. One bank account had now been canceled, and one request for a marriage license, via Gilchrist, revoked.

Holding her safe in his arms brought such peace to his soul. There might be a madwoman out there, but he'd never allow her to get to his woman. He pressed his lips to her forehead then drifted down and kissed each closed eyelid. "I wish I could strike a new deal with you."

"Ben?" Saria yawned and stretched.

"I'm here. You fell asleep on me."

"Oh, sorry." Her lids lifted and she smiled, so sweetly he wanted to spill everything he felt for her in his heart. "I didn't get as much sleep last night as I should have. I missed having my bodyguard at my back."

"I missed you too." Damn. He shouldn't have said that.

"Yes, but I missed you in ways you probably don't want to know about." She slid a finger between two of his shirt buttons and he almost purred at the delicious touch. "I can't believe I lost the first job I ever got."

"You can get back to work once Mia Taita's taken care of. Until then, you should relax and enjoy this extended break in the islands, compliments of the Whitehall family."

"I hope Tyler's brothers don't mind the change in plans."

"They'd do anything to ensure you two remained safe." So would he, and getting the girls to the other side of the island, was his priority. Yes, even should Mia Taita manage to unearth the information he'd now buried and discover their location, it was unlikely she'd consider they'd moved only a short distance away.

"Hey, you're worrying again." She popped a button and spread her hand wider over his chest. "I could help with releasing that tension if you'd like. There's one physical activity in particular which works a real treat."

"If it's one of those ways I don't want to know about, don't mention it." He stood and set her on her feet. "It's getting late. I'll take you downstairs to your room."

"Great," she grunted. "I'm a prisoner in my own room again."

* * * *

Saria leaned against her bedroom window as the setting sun sent a wash of red and gold blazing over the beach and the sweeping canopy of palm and coconut trees. Along the wharf, a crewmember freed the coiled mooring rope and the ship's motor rumbled and they moved out of their berth. Her reality had well and truly sunk in and sent her mood spiraling further downhill. "I can't believe we're going into hiding again. This is the pits."

"It's a temporary measure. Think of it only that way." Ben stood like as shadow behind her. "Why don't you get ready for dinner?"

"I'm not hungry." The last thing she wanted was food on her anxious stomach, and that short nap she'd taken earlier on Ben's lap hadn't been nearly long enough. "I might take a shower then call it a day."

"Are you sure?"

"Absolutely. You can go and boss someone else around for

the night." She strode toward the bathroom then stopped and sent him a small smile over her shoulder. "I'll catch you later."

"I want to make sure you're settled. I'll change and come back."

Ben would never leave her, not if he thought she needed him. "Okay." She nodded and closed the bathroom door.

Under the hot spray, she washed her hair then let the jets work their wonder on her tense shoulders. Finished, she dried herself and dressed in pink sleep-shorts and a white camisole. She left the bathroom and found Ben had already returned. He'd changed into black pants and a striped black and gold shirt only partially buttoned and leaving half his glorious chest on display.

His blue gaze followed her from the couch where he lay sprawled on top of a borrowed beige blanket from the end of her bed. He set his unopened book down and crossed his arms behind his pillowed head. "I ordered a dinner tray from the chef. The food should be here soon."

"I'm still not hungry." She swept her bedcovers aside and crawled in under the thin cotton sheet. "What's the book you've got?"

"A crime mystery. I grabbed it from the entertainment room upstairs. I figured I'd need something to do since the last time I hit the sack at seven would've been when I was seven."

A knock sounded.

"Great. That'll be dinner." Ben strode to door, opened it and took the tray from Henry who was decked as professionally as always in his crew whites. "Thank you."

"You're welcome, sir. Enjoy your evening."

Ben bumped the door shut with his hip, returned to the coffee table and set the tray down. The scents of fried chicken and sweet potato floated toward her, although as delicious as she knew the food would be, it didn't inspire her hunger.

"I ordered a large portion, enough for us both." He peered at her from the couch as he bit into his chicken. "You should try this. The chicken tastes almost as good as what you make."

"The chef's a trained professional. I'm sure his chicken is far superior." She plumped her pillow and rested back.

"There's blueberry cheesecake as well, another of your favorites." He lifted the plate holding a large slice with a mound of fresh blueberries on top and several rolling freely beside it.

"It looks yum." She slumped back down.

"Please, Saria. Come and eat something. It's not like you to forego a meal." He patted the space next to him. "And don't make me come over there and get you."

"I'd like to see you try."

"That sounded like a dare." With feline grace, he stood then prowled with complete silence toward her. He plucked the sheet away, slid his hands underneath her and stopped. His breath came harder as he gazed at the lacy silk outlining her breasts. "This wasn't the best idea. I should have made you walk."

"Since you're here, you can carry me." She wrapped her arms around his neck before he could let her go. He would worry if she didn't at least try to have a few bites, and she could surely manage that.

He carried her to the couch and settled her next to him. After cutting a sliver of chicken, he forked it into her mouth. "I don't want you to worry."

"I'm worried when you worry."

"What's upsetting you the most?"

"Everything. Me. You. Particularly you." She relaxed her cheek against his shoulder. He had the biggest heart and cared far more than he'd ever let anyone know. If only he'd let himself experience all life had to offer. He'd shared his past with her, Brigs, and Tyler. Now he needed to be pushed to take that next step.

Memories stirred of the first time she'd pushed herself in that way. She'd been young, just a child when she'd found an abandoned puppy in town. She'd adopted it as her own, and nothing had made her happier than watching the animal grow strong as she'd nurtured it back to health. That could be what Ben needed. Something to love and cherish, that wouldn't encroach on his decision to go it alone.

"Why are you worried about me?" His words were whisper-soft as he stroked the back of her head.

"You're so good at looking after others, but you need to have something that's all yours. What about caring for an animal? Their companionship and love heals the heart."

He snorted. "My heart is completely fine."

"Your heart's taken a beating over the years, and you should get a pet, maybe a dog. They are supposed to be man's best friend."

"Open up. You need to eat." He fed her a forkful of sweet potato then scooped a mouthful for himself.

She held up a hand so he couldn't force her to eat anything more until she'd said what she needed to. "I hate the thought of you being alone."

"I'm never alone, and since I live in the city and I'm away from home most of the time, looking after a dog wouldn't suit."

"Then I'll look after your dog whenever you're away. I love dogs."

"That doesn't take care of the city part."

"There are dogs everywhere, including the city." Maybe he needed more than a small push. "I think either a Labrador or a German shepherd would suit you. Those breeds make great guard dogs. You could train the animal and take it on duty with you." Stifling a yawn, she picked up the cheesecake and slid a spoonful into her mouth.

"If I got a pet, a goldfish would be my limit."

"A goldfish is good. I hear they don't argue back. You'd be in your element." She yawned again, set the cheesecake down and stood. "I'll get you one."

"You've only had a few bites. Sit."

"I really am tired, and I need sleep more than food, particularly if I want a clear head to keep up with you tomorrow." She crossed to her bed and flopped down.

"It's my job to ensure your welfare." Ben thumped his plate on the coffee table and stomped after her. "You're making that hard, Saria."

"Why are you so angry?"

"I'm frustrated, not angry." He pulled the sheet over her and hovered. "I don't want you thinking too much about what's happened today."

"I'll try." She stretched her tired muscles and settled as he arched one brow. "Stay with me if it makes you feel better."

He crossed his arms and tapped them as he eyed the other side of her bed.

"I promise not to pounce."

"Ha. I've heard that before, but I'll stay, provided you remain on your side." He marched around the bed, kicked off his shoes and rolled in beside her. "This'll be no different to the old times we shared."

"Yeah, but I prefer the new times, where I get to touch you, at my leisure." She snuggled against him, and unable to help herself, flicked his remaining shirt buttons open. "You'll be too hot with this on."

"You're pouncing."

"I haven't even begun to pounce yet." She eased the soft fabric apart and exposed the heavy muscle of his chest. "I didn't tell you, but while you were speaking to Dr. Hika, I snuck out to the pharmacy."

"What for?"

"I bought a couple boxes of condoms. I didn't want to be without some form of protection if you ever changed your mind. They're in my purse, right on top of the side table next to you."

"Old times means no sex." Though his gaze narrowed on her purse and his fingers flexed as if he wanted to reach for it.

"Then say no, and make it quick." She caressed his flat nipples then trailed down over each ridged ab and along his trim waist.

"I can't risk getting any more emotionally involved with you, Saria."

"We connected emotionally a long time ago, but if you'd like let's strike a new deal. We could agree to a simple fling, one which is all about the sex and nothing else."

"There's always something else when sex is involved."

"Not if we don't spend any time together outside of this bedroom. We'd never date or go out with each other."

"You're saying what happens here, stays here. That it's nights only?"

"Exactly. You could consider us friends with benefits."

"I'd need a timeframe."

"Is that a yes?" Her heartbeat pounded.

"It depends on the timeframe."

"What about whatever time remains for us here on board?" Buzzing and jiggling, she kissed the corner of his lips. "All I want is for you to live free of the burden of paying for your father's sins. You should be able to experience life as everyone else does, even though you've made the commitment to going it alone."

"In that case, yes."

"Are you sure?" She bounced onto her knees.

"Yes, because quite frankly, I don't think I can tell you no again." He shoved his shirt off, grabbed her purse and withdrew a box. "I ache for you, and the need to be inside you is all-consuming."

"Well, I'm wide awake now and ready to deal with that ache." She unbuttoned, unzipped, and removed his pants. His erect shaft lifted the waistband of his black and gray striped boxers and she traced the tip of his cock through the silky fabric. "I can't believe you said yes."

"I need to feel your touch everywhere." He cupped her cheeks in his hands. "I crave it, like the worst addiction."

"Some addictions can be good." She tugged his boxers off, encircled his cock with one hand and gently palmed his balls with the other.

His breath whooshed out and he arched off the bed. "Hell, everything feels so sensitive."

"That's because you've been denied my personal approach of healing for too long. Never again." She licked him from root to tip then swirled her tongue over the head.

"Let me undress you." He tossed her camisole away and hauled her sleep-shorts and panties off. Caressing her breasts, he rubbed his thumbs over her nipples. "So beautiful. I've missed the taste of you."

"Thank you for saying yes." She kissed him, sweeping her tongue inside his mouth until his breathing became as ragged as hers and the air thick with the heat pounding from them.

He tipped her in beside him, tore a foil packet open and made quick work of rolling it on. "I want you on your hands and knees. It's one fantasy you've yet to fulfill."

"Yes, sir. I'm all for fulfilling fantasies." She moved into position, her hair sliding off her back and over her shoulder as she grinned back at him. His cock rose higher and harder and she longed to have him buried deep within her.

He crowded her from behind, opened her folds and stroked along her slit. The heat of his chest on her back as he eased against her was a treasure all unto itself. Then he grazed his teeth along her neck and whispered in her ear, "Do you want me?"

"Yes, I want all of you."

"I want you too." He clasped her hips, pushed his cock between her legs and before she could draw her next breath, he plunged deep inside her.

He took her hard, just as she needed and pined for, and she urged him on, pushing her bottom into his groin each time he thrust forward. With his breathing and hers loud in her ears, her inner muscles tightened, locked and squeezed him in place. His passion took her soaring, her body putty in his hands as she shuddered with ecstasy. He grunted and came right along with her, and together they collapsed onto the mattress, his body a blanket of warmth across her back.

"Saria?" Her name was a warm breathy word in her ear. "Look at me. I need to see your eyes."

She threaded her fingers through his where his hand flopped over hers on the pillow. After wriggling up an inch, she rolled over and faced him. "Better?"

"Thank you." He kissed her, so sweetly she melted under his loving touch. "Are you ready for round two?"

"Always."

Chapter 9

"I'm glad these sensors finally arrived." Ben tossed another device to Tyler through the tight gap in the jungle's trees. It had been a week since they'd dropped anchor at the cove, and the first order for the alarms Gilchrist had sent had gotten lost somewhere along the way. This batch though, he'd collected personally from the resort after they'd been choppered in.

"It'll make protecting the girls go a lot easier knowing every route is covered." Kneeling, Tyler wiped his sweaty brow as he secured the sensor low on the trunk's base. He checked the camera attached to it before flipping the switch. "This one's set."

Ben mounted his last sensor in the bow of a tree, made sure he'd aimed it in the right direction so even at that height it'd catch any movement and an image. Carefully, he backed out of the scrub and returned to the trail. The dozen alarmed devices they'd set within their small corner of the island were evenly spaced out and each would send a warning to their cell phones if triggered.

"Let's head back. Lydia doesn't like it when I'm late." Tyler tracked toward the cove and Ben followed. As they made the curved white sand beach with its jagged cliffs either side, the sun dipped along the horizon and sent a final flare of red across the sky. Tyler strode to the beached inflatable and heaved it into the water.

Ben splashed through the surf, bounded into the craft and sat at the stern. He pulled the motor's cord and the engine roared to life. They were off, cruising back to the ship moored in the deep.

Once on board, Tyler walked toward Brigs as he leaned against the front glass doorway watching them, his corded binoculars swinging around his neck. Tyler clapped Brigs on the back and disappeared inside.

Ben stopped next to Brigs. "How are the girls?"

"They had an enjoyable day. Saria went diving with Dylan and Luke this afternoon, and Lydia kicked back by the pool with Liam and Nico. They're below-stairs now, getting ready for dinner."

For the past week, Ben had kept his word in his and Saria's bargain. Nights only. He'd steered clear of her during the day, allowing Brigs or Tyler to watch her. Which had been damn hard and only just doable.

"I've got some news." Brigs cleared his throat.

"Good or bad?"

"Good. Agent Gilchrist called. Mia Taita is still holed up in her gated seaside Wellington home, but he's managed to get a team in when she wasn't looking and her place is now bugged."

"About time we got in there. The woman has to slip up sooner or later, and Gilchrist needs to catch her."

"She's a sly one, always getting others to do her dirty work for her. Gilchrist is now more prepared. He's tackling every angle he can."

"So are we. Check your cell phone. Make sure it's picking up the activated sensors."

Brigs lugged it out of his pocket. "They're showing." He eyed him. "Does this mean you're happy for the girls to roam the beach if they'd like to?"

"Absolutely. They've been looking forward to stretching their legs on land."

"So have Tyler's brothers. Even on board, they hover over them, never letting them out of their sight."

No surprises there. The urge to keep them safe buzzed through all of them. "I'll see you at dinner."

"You're actually going to make it tonight?" Brigs cocked a disbelieving brow.

"Yeah, good point. I might see you at dinner." He couldn't trot downstairs fast enough. Once inside their room, he flicked the lock.

The bathroom door opened and steam billowed out. Saria stood there with a delectable smile on her lips and not one inch of her gloriously creamy skin covered. Well, apart from her wet hair clinging to her breasts and hiding those luscious nipples.

"You're right on time. I've just got back from diving and turned the shower on." She sashayed toward him, gripped his hem and lifted his shirt over his head. "Did you have a good day?"

"Yes, I'm one very happy bodyguard with alarmed sensors in place." After shucking his cargo shorts, he walked her backward into the bathroom. He swung her into the shower, pinned her against the glass side and kissed her as he'd longed to all day. Hot water pummeled his shoulders, and his woman slid her arms around his neck and held on. He relaxed, every tense muscle easing as peace invaded his soul.

"I love the way you hold me. It makes me feel so secure, cherished, and wanted. Even when you're inside me, I can feel your strength and determination, along with such sweet tenderness." She hooked one leg behind his knee, rubbed up and down his calf. "Sorry, I don't mean to get all sentimental."

"That's in your nature. As long as you don't make anything more out of our agreement than what we've decided, you can get as sentimental as you like." He cupped her bottom and drew her hard against him.

"I won't make a thing out of it. The sex is hot, and that's

what I like." She nibbled his neck. "Brigs told us about the call from Gilchrist, that Mia Taita's place is now bugged."

"We'll catch her."

"I know you will."

Her faith in him was absolute, something he valued beyond belief. "Tell me about the diving."

"We explored along the reef, but I got distracted by the dolphins." Her tone bubbled with excitement. "One nudged Luke to the surface. He grabbed its fin and it took him for a ride. It was the most amazing sight."

Luke was damn lucky to have spent the day with Saria. "Tomorrow, you're welcome to use the beach." That way he could watch her, even if from a distance.

"Wonderful. Nico is bursting to build a sandcastle. Lydia's actually drawn up a master plan for one." She glided her hands down his sides as she slowly knelt. "Pass me the soap."

His already hard cock got incredibly harder. "I'm not—"

She slid her lips around him then licked the head.

"—going to last if you do that."

"That's your fault for being so tasty." One mischievous wink and she sucked him deep into her mouth. Oh hell, he was a goner.

* * * *

Saria intended to tempt Ben beyond his endurance. On her knees, with the water sluicing down her body, she built his pleasure with her mouth until his thighs shook and his fingers pressed deep into her shoulders.

He groaned and rocked his hips. "Please, Saria. Show me some mercy."

"Mercy is completely overrated."

"I want to be inside of you, not to come in your mouth." He pulled out and sagged against the shower wall. "Hell, that was one of the hardest things I've ever done."

Yet harder still was his cock and she was without a

condom. "Wait here, Ben. I didn't think of protection."

"No, I'm not letting you go now. We'll come back and finish this shower later." He scooped her into his arms and carried her dripping wet body to the bed. He tumbled her onto the mattress, nabbed what he needed from the bedside table and sheathed himself.

"You forgot to turn the water off."

"If you've got time to think about that, then I'm not doing my job properly." His gaze roamed over her chest then he crawled on top of her, cupped her breasts and eased them together. Slowly, he licked her nipple. The hot stroke of his tongue sent a bolt of desire to her core, and all thought of the running water flitted from her mind.

"I love when you kiss me like that."

"I've only just begun." He grinned then nipped the tip.

"Show me." He did, sucking her nipple deep into his mouth until a torrent of tingles raced through her. She grabbed his arms and clung. "That feels so good."

"For me too." He swept her legs apart and knelt between them. "Now to make you feel even better."

"Everything you do makes me feel that way." Up on her elbows, she traced the ridged bands of his stomach. His hard muscles were honed to perfection, and his abs rippled as she brushed the head of his cock. His shaft was thick and long and saluting her from a thatch of blond hair, the same pale color as his head. She sat straighter, bringing their bodies closer together. His chest hair tickled her breasts and she sighed with delight. Then he kissed her, hot and hard and exactly as she wanted. She loved his kisses.

He broke for air, blue eyes twinkling. Then he drifted lower, kissing and licking. She fell back onto the bed as he bent his head and kissed along her inner thighs, his breath puffing against her skin. He dipped his finger along her folds then rubbed her clit.

"Please, yes please." She grabbed fistfuls of the soft cotton bed sheet. "More."

"Demand anything you wish." He plunged one finger deep inside her then stroked, harder and faster, until he hit that spot which had her gasping.

"I want you buried deep inside me and to never leave." She looked into his eyes as she skimmed his cock. She caressed his hot flesh then pumped him in time with how he stroked her. "Now."

"As you wish." He slid over top of her and filled her completely.

"Ben." She writhed as he thrust and melded their bodies together. Each of his deeply penetrating strokes took her over. "I can't hold on any longer."

"Then don't."

"Only with you." The words rushed from her as blissful spasm after spasm racked her body, and he came too, his climax tumbling over hers and sending her flying into oblivion.

"You okay?"

"Mmm," she mumbled. "Never better."

Chapter 10

Later that week, having handed the communications to Brigs for the day, Ben patrolled the cove in the hope of having Saria in his sight for a while. She and Lydia, along with Liam, had Nico buzzing about as another of their monster sandcastles took form. They'd built so many, one each day and they dotted the white sand of their private beach. He stepped out from under the shady tree line. Out in the bay, one of the inflatable's motors roared to life and Tyler pulled away from the ship. He cruised in and beached the craft next to the two WaveRunners Dylan and Luke had been blasting about on earlier.

Tyler jogged toward him. "Hey, another update just came in from Gilchrist. One of his techs found a backdoor into Taita Software's network." Gilchrist was working every angle he could.

"Has he found anything of interest?" With Taita Software being one of the most secure networks in the country, as yet they'd found very little.

"No, but he'll let us know how it goes."

After two weeks of no movement in their case, the whole team felt the pressure to uncover the solid evidence they needed to toss Mia's butt back behind bars.

Ben loosened the back zip of his wetsuit an inch and ran his finger around the tight neckline. He should head out and do another sweep along the cliffs since Tyler was back.

"You look anxious." Tyler crossed his arms.

"It's nothing." No one-on-one time with Saria during the day sucked, particularly when she was in sight. "Go and spend some time with your girl." At least Tyler could.

"Thanks. Take it easy, okay?" Tyler strode toward Lydia as she collected a bucket of water from the surf. She and Saria had built a wide moat around Nico's sandcastle. Lydia sloshed the water in and Liam gave a jubilant shout from the center of the massive structure then high-fived Saria. The two laughed and then hugged Nico who snuck out of their embrace and danced around them in his red swim shorts.

"This is the best sandcastle ever." Nico giggled.

Never had Ben experienced a childhood like that, where attention was lavished so freely on one. He'd missed out on so much, and being around Tyler's family these past few weeks had only nailed that knowledge home.

Saria left the others, wandered toward the surf and rubbed the sand from her knees. The incoming tide splashed her white shorts and she gripped the elastic waistband. Hell, she was going for a swim. He should turn away, only it was impossible. She shimmied her shorts off and kicked them up onto the dry sand, a move so sensuous, his mouth watered. Slowly running her fingers under the lower edge of her red bikini bottoms, she straightened the shiny fabric.

Not going to her made every nerve in his body stretch to breaking point. He wanted to touch her, but instead he remained right where he was as she stepped into the water, lifted her gloriously long brown locks and stretched her body. The two squares of red material hugging her breasts strained over the mounds and he gritted his teeth. When she finally walked deeper, dove and disappeared beneath the water's surface, he released his breath.

He waited for her to appear, and like a sea nymph, she rose

with water running down her body. A loud laugh burst from her, and then she grabbed her foot.

Luke emerged from under the water, lifted her up and tossed her. Dylan was out there too, both of them snorkeling after their jet ski.

She came up for air, shoved against Luke's chest and pushed him backward. The two disappeared within the water's depths, and unable to hold back any longer, Ben strode into the waves. As she resurfaced, with Luke's mask and snorkel in hand, she slid it on and dived with a last laugh.

"Saria!" Luke yelled. "Get back here now, you vixen."

"Hey, Luke." He joined the man. "You need me to grab your gear?"

"No, I'll go and fetch another set from the inflatable. I didn't get a chance to warn her though. The tide's turning and it's rough out near the reef."

"I'll keep an eye on her." Her safety and wellbeing came first, even over their agreement. He swam toward her before she got too far, dived and snagged her hand. As she jerked around, he pointed upward and she nodded her understanding.

They broke the surface together and she eased the snorkel's mouthpiece to one side. "What's up, Hammers?"

When she said his last name like that, it always got him so hard. Now was no exception. "The tide's turning."

"That tends to happen a couple of times a day, so far as I know." Grinning, she tweaked his nose. "Do you have anything else enlightening to add?"

"Luke said it's rough. It's best I swim with you." He kept a stern expression, even though he wanted to smile at her cheekiness.

"Since when do I need a guardian in the water?" Her curious frown sent a buzz of need through him, and he was already needy enough.

"It's a precaution, and it won't hurt you to take it." The

waves bumped them together and he caught her around the waist. "Please, Saria."

"I gave you my word. No time together outside of the bedroom. Let me honor that. Send Tyler out to watch me if you're that concerned." She popped her snorkel back in and kicked away. Damn it, he needed this, to remain with her. He'd certainly had enough of missing her when she was so close.

It was time for them to speak about it. He dived. Colorful fish darted about as he searched for her within the deep blue. A partial reef between them and the ship formed a natural underwater reserve, one she loved snorkeling along. That could be where she'd gone. He surfaced, wiped his eyes and got his bearings.

"Ben!" Saria screamed his name from a hundred feet away.

He was off, powering through the water toward her. He grabbed her arms as she dropped beneath the waves. Blood sloshed all around as he hauled her close and removed her mask. "Where are you hurt?"

"My back, up high." Her eyelids fluttered shut, and a stingray splashed the surface and shot away.

Heart pounding, he swam them both back toward the shore.

"What happened?" Tyler raced into the water as he carried Saria in, Lydia right behind him. On her front, Ben laid her down, her head carefully turned to the side.

Blood oozed from a gaping wound on her back. "A stingray attacked her." He pressed the ragged edges together.

Lydia fell to her knees and checked Saria's breathing. "She's out of it. Open your eyes, sis."

She remained unresponsive and Ben nudged Lydia. "Get the first aid kit. Some clean water and towels. Everything should be in the inflatable. Move quickly."

"I won't be a sec." She raced, yelling at Liam to keep Nico away.

Tyler inspected the wound. "For her to suffer a strike so

high on her body, the stingray had to have been swimming above her. She would have been caught unaware."

"I saw it splash away along the water's surface. We'll wrap this up, take her straight to the doctor. Can you go and get the boat ready for me?"

"Sure thing." Tyler dashed off.

Saria moaned and squirmed. "Ben?"

"I'm here, baby. Stay still."

"It hurts." Her eyes flickered open and she squeezed his leg where he knelt near her head. "You're pressing too hard."

He eased back on the pressure, but only a touch. "That better?"

"A little. How bad is it?" Her chilled fingers shook on his thigh.

"The wound's a couple of inches long. Tyler's getting the inflatable ready, and we'll take you straight to the doc."

"I've got everything." Lydia skidded in, unscrewed the bottle lid and gently splashed water over the wound, rinsing the fine grains of sand away. "Trust you to take on a stingray, Saria Sands."

"I didn't even see it." Saria poked Lydia in the leg with a wobbly finger. "I'm hurt here. Don't grump at me."

"You scared me." Lydia kissed her cheek. "I'm allowed to get grumpy when that happens. I love you."

"I love you too, sis."

"I'm going to bandage the wound. It might hurt a bit." Lydia dabbed the area dry with a clean white cloth. Flinching, Saria closed her eyes and gripped his leg. He desperately wanted to hold her, to take away her pain.

"It'll be okay, Ben." Lydia nodded at him as if understanding what he felt. "Move your fingers out of the way as I bind it." He did and she carefully taped Saria's flesh together, applied a sterile pad and fixed it firmly in place. To her sister, she said, "What I've done should hold until the doctor can stitch it."

"Thank you." Saria glanced at him. "Can you help me put my shorts on?"

"Sure." He slid them on then scooped her up, and mindful of her back, carried her high against his chest to where Tyler waited with the inflatable. On board, he cradled her in his lap as Tyler revved the motor and sped them out of the bay toward the resort. He kissed the top of her head. "How does your back feel?"

"Better now it's taped." As they bumped over the waves, she cringed and tried to hold still. "I'm sorry. I didn't mean to get hurt. I just wanted to keep my promise."

"This is my fault. I shouldn't have let you swim away. We need to strike a new deal." He tipped her chin up, melded his mouth to hers and luxuriated in the feel of being with her. "I can't lose you."

"I guess it wouldn't look so hot on your résumé if you lost a client."

"I didn't mean—" The craft crested a massive wave. He lifted her as the hull slammed down. The impact knocked the wind from his lungs, but thankfully he'd kept her from the brunt of it.

"Are you okay?" She fluttered her fingers over his chest as spray blew over them.

"I'm fine. Hold tight. Tyler's in a hurry."

They rounded the final bend toward the wharf and relief poured through him.

Tyler slowed and guided the inflatable up onto the shore, clambered out and called, "I'll go and let the doctor know what's happened and that you're on your way."

"Do that. Fast." With Saria in his arms, he stepped out and strode toward the doctor's clinic as Tyler disappeared along the coral sandstone path ahead.

"You should let me walk." Saria frowned as he crossed the

bridged walkway over a garden-edged pond. "We're attracting a lot of attention, and you've spent the past two weeks ensuring I remain invisible."

"Then hide your head, because I've no intention of putting you down." He should've instructed Tyler to bring them in via the beach's side access near the meadow.

"Stubborn man." With an arm wrapped around his neck, she dipped her head in close against his throat and nipped his skin. Heat raced through his veins as memories surged of her sucking the same spot last night. Hell, he needed her, and not just sexually. Something he'd have to address and soon.

At the clinic door, Tyler waved him in and he quickly forced his thoughts back into order.

"Dr. Hika's in the rear surgical room," Tyler instructed. "His last appointment for the day just left, and the area's clear."

"Thanks." He marched inside and Tyler shut and locked the door with a snick. In the back room with its white walls, labeled cupboards, and shiny metal countertop, he gently set Saria down on a white-sheeted medical bed.

Dr. Hika stepped in front of Saria and stared into her eyes. "Tyler told me a stingray caught you across the back, and that you lost consciousness for a minute or so."

"She did," Ben answered for her. "Her sister taped and bandaged the wound as best as she could."

"I'll take a look." The doctor pulled a tray of utensils forward, hastened around to the other side of the bed and removed the bandage Lydia had applied. "There aren't any barbs, Saria, but I'll need to clean this wound properly then I'll stitch it. I'll numb the area first. You'll feel a pinch as the injection goes in."

"It's all right. I know the drill." Knuckles white, she gripped the edge of the thin mattress. Ben rubbed her knee and she squeezed his hand. "I'm okay."

"You won't be okay until you're healed."

"Well, technically speaking, yes, but I'm still okay."

Long minutes passed then finally the doctor applied a sterile bandage over the area. "Saria, you'll need to keep these stitches dry for the next five days, and I'll issue you with a prescription for pain relief. You can start the meds immediately. Follow the prescription for dosage."

"Thank you." Saria flinched. "And pain meds sound good."

He wrote on his pad, tore the sheet off and handed it to Tyler. "Drop this into the pharmacy so they can fill it before they shut at five. The wait's usually ten or fifteen minutes."

"Will do." Tyler eyed Ben. "I'll return the moment it's done."

"If you have to wait for it, then run and move the inflatable around to the beach entrance on the meadow's side. It's quieter. I should have mentioned it before."

"I know the entrance you're talking about. I'll lock the door as I leave." Striding out, Tyler patted the weapon holstered under his shirt.

The doctor dropped his utensils into the automated cleaning machine on the bench then returned to Saria and gave her a smile. "How do you feel now?"

"Woozy. Sore." Sweat beaded along her brow.

"As a precaution, I want someone to wake you every hour or two during the night." The doctor glanced at him. "I also need to check the wound again first thing in the morning. Don't worry about making an appointment. Just come straight in. I understand you're trying to lay low."

"Thanks, Doc. I appreciate everything you've done."

"No problem." His cell phone beeped and he checked the display. "Sorry, I've got another emergency down by the pool. I have to go, but stay as long as you need to." The doctor flicked the lock as he raced out the door.

"I guess that means you're on night duty." Saria wriggled forward and he cupped her hips and helped her off the bed and onto her feet.

"I'll gladly wake you every hour or two, although possibly not for the reason I wanted to." He guided her to one of the gray metal chairs in the waiting room. "We'll remain here until Tyler returns. Keep you out of sight."

She rolled her shoulders and cried out. "Ow, I can't do that. The wound is right between my shoulder blades where I want to stretch."

"Then don't." He clasped her hands and looked into her eyes. "We need to talk."

"If you're going to ban me from swimming forever, then I'm not listening."

"I'd never do that." He lifted her hand and pressed a kiss against her palm. "Although you're not allowed to go swimming without me."

"Should you be doing that? It's still daylight for another hour and kissing is supposed to be off-limits then."

"Which is what I wanted to talk to you about earlier."

"I remember. Losing a client isn't a good look." Groaning, she closed her eyes. "It still hurts. Do you think you could run over to the pharmacy and sweet talk one of the staff into handing over my meds now?"

That wasn't what he'd been about to say, but it could wait. "We'll talk as soon as I get back." He locked the door, dashed across to the pharmacy and approached the uniformed saleswoman stocking a shelf. "I'm after Saria Sands' meds, please. It's urgent."

"The pharmacist is still preparing them. I'll go and tell him to put a hurry on it. Won't be long." She walked into the back room.

Anxious to head right back to Saria, he tapped the dark blue countertop next to the till and forced himself to stand and wait. Their current agreement needed a change, one that would give him more time with her and ensure she never got hurt again.

She was his to protect. She always had been, and always would be.

* * * *

The stinging pain radiated out and throbbed deep down into Saria's spine. If only that injection had numbed more than the wound's immediate site. Tangling with a stingray wasn't something she ever intended to do again, or seeing the pain her injury had caused Ben. His gaze had been haunted, and without a doubt, she knew he blamed himself for what had happened to her.

A knock sounded and relief poured through her. "Coming, Ben." Trembling, she rose to her feet, fumbled with the lock and opened the door.

"Are you Lydia Sands?" A broad-shouldered man with shaggy brown hair and beady black eyes loomed over her. "Or are you the other twin, Saria Sands?"

"I—I'm Saria."

He pushed her backward and slammed the door shut. Exposed on his bulky bicep was a large tattoo of a hyena, blood dripping from its sharp-toothed jaws. "About time I found one of you two. Now, I need to stash you somewhere so I can get to your sister. Mia sent me after Lydia, and you're gonna be my bait. Say nighty-night." He shoved a rag over her mouth and nose.

She gagged and the room spun. Black dots danced before her eyes, then nothing.

Chapter 11

Agonized, Ben strode into the resort's security control room where Tyler continued to comb through the recorded surveillance. Twenty-four heart-wrenching hours had passed since Saria had been abducted, and they didn't seem to be any further ahead in their search for her than they'd been in the first hour. "We had so many damn checks in place," he snapped as he sank into the chair next to Tyler's. "How the hell did someone sneak onto this island without an alert being raised?"

"With patience and cunning, but we'll find her." Tyler kept his gaze on the monitor, not missing a beat. "Where's Officer Kupita?"

"The wharf, supervising the shift change and ensuring those men he has heading out across the island are all updated. I warned him about the alarmed sensors we have wired around the cove." He tapped the screen. "Are you looking at the footage out by the main entrance again?"

"Yep. Someone slipped past us both, when you were right next door, and I came through the front foyer only a minute or two after you left her. Whoever took her moved fast. Damn fast. The evidence has to be here somewhere." Tyler scraped his chair back, grabbed another disk from the overhead shelf and inserted it. "How's Gilchrist doing? Heard any word from him this afternoon?"

"Not in the past two hours. He's still working methodically through the resort's manifest, double checking what I've already checked." No one could make a resort booking without a confirmed passport number, and when visitors arrived, their passports were verified. That included all passengers from the ferry or the moored ships. It was standard practice, and usually sufficient, yet something had gone terribly wrong for someone who should have raised a red flag to sneak in without their knowledge.

Unable to sit still, Ben pushed his chair back and stood. "I'm going to run another perimeter check. Call me if you see anything suspicious, and I don't care how minor it is."

"I just wish they had more cameras where it counted." Tyler jumped forward. "Wait. Take a look at this footage. It doesn't cover the main building but the staff service area at the rear of the property."

The image showed a shaggy brown-haired male around his mid-thirties pushing a wheeled laundry basket out of the service elevator. His yellow staff polo pulled tight across his back and sat far too short on his body. In place of yellow uniform shorts, he wore black pants with a triple white side stripe.

Tyler motioned toward the printer. "A copy's coming through for you now, and I'll email the image to Gilchrist for facial recognition."

"Send a copy to Kupita as well. Have him distribute it among his men. About damn time we got something." Ben nabbed the picture before the ink had even dried. "I've not seen this man at any of the staff or security meetings, and he'd be hard to miss. Does the camera footage show where he's headed?"

"I'll check that now." Tyler released the pause button.

The man rolled his basket overflowing with towels and linens past the laundry doors. He disappeared from sight around the far corner. The service area was made up of a two-story block that bordered the far side of the meadow. Thick gardens and bush between the main building and that one kept most of it from the public's view. "I'll head over to the laundry now and run a visual." He raced out the door with the picture in hand. This was the strongest lead they'd had so far.

Saria had to be alive.

He needed his woman back.

Now.

* * * *

Hot. So hot. Saria opened her lids and sweat dribbled into her eyes and hazed her vision. She blinked and squinted toward a sliver of light shining on the strangest angle.

She tried to move her arms and legs, but only managed to tighten the bindings around her ankles and wrists, both roped together behind her and making her arch backward as she lay on her side. Her back and shoulders throbbed, and her head thumped as if drums beat within.

Pushing with her tongue, she tried to spit out the foul-tasting gag, but another piece of fabric around it held it firmly in place. Her stomach rolled and she dry heaved. She had to get out of here, wherever here was.

No windows, and the space was cramped. A broken shovel and a dusty broom lay propped near her head against the tin wall, both covered in spider webs.

While trying to move, she scratched her shoulder against the pitted concrete floor. Dark and all-consuming pain raked through her. Tears streaked down her cheeks and puddled on the floor. She shouldn't have opened that stupid door when she knew the rules. Ben would be blaming himself for leaving her alone. Oh, and Lydia. Her poor sister would be beside herself. "I need you, Ben," she mumbled into the cloth. "Find me, please."

She gritted her teeth and pushed through the searing pain of trying to loosen the bindings.

* * * *

Ben stormed along the concrete terrace toward the service elevator, the photograph in hand. Mimicking the assailant's movements, he continued past the laundry doors then strode around the corner.

Two flights of steps led down to the meadow, while along the building's back boundary, the jungle rose thick and strong. Within that dense area, miles upon miles of prime hiding space, lay.

He tapped the image. That waist-high canvas laundry basket was large enough to hold Saria, but he'd have been unable to roll it downstairs.

Across the meadow, a gardener was deadheading red and pink flowering hibiscus bushes, tossing clippings into his wheelbarrow. Ben jogged downstairs and over to the man in green overalls. "Excuse me. A woman has gone missing, and we're looking for this man. He would have been in this area around five yesterday afternoon. Have you seen anyone of his—"

A dull clatter resonated somewhere within the trees. The hairs on his arms rose, and his senses flared to full alert.

The gardener set his clippers down and peered into the bushes at an old tin shed covered in ivy. "That's old Wiri's shed. I haven't used that for storage in years. Sounds like something dinged against it."

"I'll check it out." Ben shoved through the brush. A boulder was wedged against the door. He rolled it clear and turned the shed's rusty knob. The door creaked as he hauled it open. Musty air assailed him and on the concrete floor inside, a trickle of light played over a woman's body.

"Saria?" His heart lurched. He fell to his knees and pressed two fingers against her neck. Her pulse beat weakly. She had to have just been awake, enough to make that noise. Now, she lay completely unresponsive, soaked with sweat. Bruises mottled her arms and legs, and her shoulders were red and raw. As carefully as he could, he removed the bindings contorting her back into a painful arch then untied the cloth around her head. Gently, he slid the stuffed rag holding a trace of chloroform out of her mouth. "I'll get you out of here, baby. And I'm never going to let you out of my sight ever again. You hear me?"

"Ben?" She moaned and tears leaked from behind her closed eyes.

He scooped her into his arms and her head lolled back, her hands swinging limply down.

"I'm taking you to the doctor now. He'll make the pain go away." With Saria tight against his chest, he raced to the main building, shouldered the control room's door open and yelled at Tyler. "I've got her."

"I'll cover you." Tyler shot to his feet, his hand on his weapon.

Ben flew into the clinic and Tyler slammed and locked the door behind them.

"You've found her." Dr. Hika slapped the wheeled bed. "Put her down, as carefully as you can."

Ben hated to let her go, but he did. "She was inside the old gardening shed at the edge of the jungle."

"I know the one. The bush grew over it years ago." The doctor checked her pupils and she flinched and cried out. "She's waking. Get some ice chips from the corner freezer. I'll get an IV hooked up. She's badly dehydrated."

Ben grabbed a plastic cup from the bench and scooped ice into it. He dribbled a chip over Saria's lips. She sighed, opened her mouth and licked his fingers.

Cradling her head, he offered her more. "Open your eyes for me, Saria."

Her lids fluttered and her beautiful brown eyes focused on him.

"Talk to me." He had to hear her voice.

"Keep wetting her throat, Ben. Give her some time." Dr.

Hika inserted the IV into her wrist then fiddled with the bag hooked onto a pole until clear fluid dripped down. He peered into her eyes. "Saria, I'm giving you some nutrients as well as pain relief in the IV. If you can, tell me where you feel the most pain."

"M-my back." Her voice was raspy. "Something's wrong. Infected."

"I'll take a look now." To Ben, he said, "Roll her onto her good shoulder, the one without the grazes and make sure she can see you at all times. I don't need her panicking."

Smoothly, Ben rolled her.

Tyler cleared his throat. "I've just sent a message to Gilchrist and Kupita to let them know what's happened, and copied it to Lydia and Brigs as well." Tyler cupped Saria's cheek. "Your sister is so worried about you."

"M-miss her," she garbled then grasped Ben's arm. "S-sorry. Didn't check. Forgot. Opened door."

"It's my fault. I should never have left you unguarded." He kissed the top of her head. "I'll never make that mistake again." On his life, he wouldn't. "Can you tell me anything about the man who took you?"

"Had hyena tattoo, like Kern and Ladd Hyena. A-after Lydia. Said Mia sent him."

"That's good." He nodded at Tyler. "Pass the information along."

"I'm onto it." Tyler's fingers flew over the keys as he sent another message.

The doctor buzzed around Saria. "The wound's definitely infected. I'll add antibiotics to your IV. How's the pain? Is it lessening?"

She mumbled and her eyelids drooped.

"Saria, no." Ben shot a look at the doctor. "Do I need to keep her awake?"

"I'm keeping an eye on her vitals. Let her sleep if she can."

Ben stroked her matted hair as her breathing evened out.

The doctor re-bandaged her wound, washed her face and shoulder and applied a salve. He checked the IV and seemed satisfied. "It'll be a long night, so feel free to pull up a chair or use the couch in my office if you need to rest."

"Thanks. We will."

The doctor gently rolled Saria onto her back and draped a sheet over her.

Ben sat next to her, his fingers firmly threaded through hers as he wished her right back to wakefulness. He pressed his lips to her ear. "If I'd lost you, I would have died. I need you, Saria, alive, and with me."

His heart ached with how much he needed her.

* * * *

Saria wriggled her trapped feet and tried to shove against whatever held her down.

"Stay still, baby. You're free and you're safe."

"Ben?" She forced her eyes open then blinked at the harsh brightness of the overhead light. Everything spun then slowly settled. She was safe, back with Ben. "Are you real?" Her voice was crap.

"I'm here."

Images assailed her, of a man with shaggy brown hair and a hyena tattoo. Dr. Hika had cared for her and Ben had fed her ice chips. Tyler had been here too. "Is Lydia okay?"

"Brigs is watching her, and she remains on the ship. Dr. Hika's just stepped out, but he'll be back in a minute or two." His gaze searched hers. "How do you feel?"

She tried to sit up, but the pressure on her bladder made her groan. "I need to use the bathroom."

"I'll take you." He grabbed the IV pole, wrapped one arm around her waist, and helped her slide off the bed and onto her feet.

"Is there any sign of the man who did this to me?" She

leaned against the solid warmth of him, her fingers bunched in his cotton shirt and her forehead pressed against his chest. He crowded her, big and tall. No one could hurt her if he was here. He'd never let them.

"No, but we'll find him. We have his image and soon we'll have his exact ID. Come on. This way." He aided her into the large rear bathroom. The overhead fan whirred and fluttered the coral-colored shower curtain.

"What time is it?" With no windows, she couldn't tell.

"It's three in the morning. You've been asleep for hours." He guided her into the separate toilet and tipped up her chin, his gaze on hers. "Leave the door unlocked so I can come in if you need me."

"Okay." Except she didn't move, hated the thought of letting go of him.

"I know," he whispered in her ear. "I'll be right outside."

"Promise me."

"I promise." Agony crossed his face as he closed the door and left her.

As quick as she could, she tended to her needs then washed her hands in the small white basin. In the oval mirror above it, the depth of her ordeal showed in her sunken eyes, pale skin, and bruised body. She plucked a twig from her hair and flicked it into the wastebasket. She was incredibly lucky Ben had found her.

"Are you all right?" He knocked then opened the door and peeked in. "Do you want to change into something clean? I found a hospital gown in the drawer under the bed."

"Yes, I smell like that cramped tin shed. I need a quick wash."

"You got it." With his hold on her firm, he ushered her toward the metal stool sitting inside the open shower cubicle. He slid her shorts down, left her bikini on then helped her sit. "We'll have to be careful we don't get your bandages wet, or the doctor won't be happy." He rolled the cuffs on his blue and black paneled shirt to the elbow then flicked the shower lever on and passed her the spray-head.

Carefully, he soaped her front and legs while she rinsed the suds away. Done, he turned the water off, wrapped her in a fluffy blue towel then knelt at her feet. Gently, reverently, he settled his head in her lap. "I need a minute. No moving for you."

"I couldn't move if I wanted to." She needed this moment too. She tangled her fingers in his hair and held onto him.

"I'm sorry, Saria, for everything." Emotion clogged his voice.

"I don't remember most of my ordeal. The chloroform kept me out of it until the gag dried out." She stroked his silky blond hair, reveling in being able to touch him as she pleased. "I shouldn't have opened that door unless I knew it was you. All I could think was 'yes, you're back.'"

"You'll have a guard no more than a step away from you going forward, and that'll be me ninety-nine percent of the time." He slid his arms around her waist, rose higher and looked into her eyes. "Can you tell me anything else about the man who took you?"

"Not much more than I already have. He said I was the bait to get to Lydia then he knocked me out with the chloroform. It was quick." She tucked a loose strand of his hair behind his ear. "When I came to, I tried to kick the shovel over."

"You managed it. I heard the clatter." He clasped her face, brought her mouth to his. His kiss was slow, tender, and brimming with emotion. All too soon though, he pulled away. "Let's get you dressed."

"What's going to happen now? Apart from the whole fulltime guard thing."

"The man's clearly after Lydia since she's the eye witness to the hit-and-run on Taita's brother. It's doubtful he'll leave this island without taking her or returning for you." He removed her towel, carefully slid the hospital gown over her damp bikini and tied the flapping sides together. "Lydia's confined again to the ship even though the cove is alarmed, and I intend to get you back to her as quick as I can. There's only guaranteed safety with the ocean between you and any more possible danger."

"Is someone watching that shed in case he returns?"

"Officer Kupita has one of his men on it."

"Will you go after him?" She clutched the pole with one hand and his arm with the other.

"Once I've taken care of you, yes. It's my job to find him, and your job to get better." Rolling her IV pole along with them, he guided her back to the surgical room. At the steel counter, Dr. Hika sat on a stool writing up notes. He glanced up as he heard them coming.

"I didn't expect you to rise so soon." He crossed to her. "How's the pain?"

"Manageable since you've got me juiced up." She tapped the IV bag.

"Yes, everything you need is in there." He helped her onto the bed and checked her temperature and vitals before replacing the bag. "You're doing great. I want you to lie down. With plenty of sleep, you'll heal quicker."

She yawned and held out her hand toward Ben. "Can I use your cell phone? I need to call Lydia."

"Of course." He pulled the bed sheet over her and made the call. "Hey, Lydia, Saria's here and demanding to talk to you." He passed her the phone.

"When have I ever been demanding, Ben?"

"Saria, is that you?" Lydia's anxious voice pounded down the line.

"Yes, it's me."

"Are you okay? Tyler said you were, but I'm so relieved you rang. When are you coming home?"

"As soon as the doc releases me. Hopefully soon. What

about you? Are you feeling okay?"

"I'll be better once you're here. How's the pain?"

"There isn't any with the meds I'm—oh." Her eyelids drooped. "The doctor's snuck a sedative in. Can't...."

"What's wrong? Stay with me."

"Can't. 'Leepy." Ben's face wavered, and she slowly shut her eyes. "Don't leave me," she whispered to him. "Need you."

"I'll always be here. Always."

The dark took her away, and from the one person she never wanted to leave.

Chapter 12

The next morning in the doctor's surgical room, Ben stirred. He rolled his shoulders and eased the crook in his neck from sleeping in the low-backed chair. Saria lay peacefully nestled on her side, one hand tucked under her cheek and her breath whispering softly between her lips. That sweet sound had finally soothed him into slumber himself.

He stretched his legs, stood and traipsed across to the doorway leading into the doctor's private office. Tyler sat in the leather swivel chair behind Dr. Hika's chunky desk, his laptop open in front of him. "Where's the doc, Tyler?"

"He dashed off to his room for a shower and a change of clothes. Said he'll be back soon to check on the patient before the clinic opens at nine."

"Anything come in from Gilchrist this morning?"

"Just now. He's identified Saria's kidnapper as Boyd Hyena. The man is Kern and Ladd Hyena's cousin and affiliated with the same Wellington gang as them. Gilchrist has a search warrant and is heading to Hyena's flat, right after he swings by to pick up Mia Taita."

"Saria's evidence is enough?"

"He hopes so, or at least until he can gather further proof."

"Good. Things are stacking up against Mia Taita." Although they needed something solid on top of Saria's word.

He folded his arms. "We need to find Hyena before he causes any more trouble."

"Kupita has doubled the number of teams searching the jungle. This place is crawling with his men."

"Ben?" Saria, in her loose hospital gown, stood in the doorway with her IV pole in hand. She rubbed her sleepy eyes with her knuckles. "I heard."

"We'll catch Boyd Hyena. I promise you that."

"I know you will." She held out a hand and he rushed across. "I need to use the bathroom again. Can you come with me? I'm not ready to go in there alone."

"You don't even need to ask." Hell, he hated she was still so scared.

"Wait up." Tyler snagged a plastic bag from the green couch and passed it to her. "Take these. I called in a favor at reception and they opened the gift shop for me. I picked out some clothes for you that should fit. They're the same size as what Lydia wears."

"Then that'll be perfect." She kissed his cheek. "Tyler, I swear you're going to make a fabulous brother-in-law, that's if you ever get married to my sister." She rolled her pole toward the bathroom as Ben walked beside her.

"Tell me what you need." He closed the bathroom door.

"A hand changing." She pulled the side ties on the gown and eased the loose fabric over her head. "Is there any underwear in that bag? The bikini's doing a fine job, but I'd love a complete change of clothes."

If Tyler had brought her underwear, he was in huge trouble. He opened the bag and growled. A pink satin bra and panties sat on top of the other purchases. The man was dead.

Saria peered into the bag and smiled. "Oh, and Tyler has good taste too."

The man was double-dead. Gruffly, he stood with the bra in hand. "How do I put this on?"

"Take a guess." She released the back ties of her bikini and her full breasts bobbed free.

He embraced one mound and rubbed his thumb over her rosy nipple. "I've missed you."

"I've missed you too, and the fabric cups that part."

"You're really going to make me dress you?"

"Absolutely." She grinned. "If you put your mind to it, I'm sure you'll manage perfectly fine."

"You're a cruel woman." He slid her bra into place then wrapped his arms around her and clipped the back hooks. He stroked the silk cups, relishing the smooth fabric and her nipples as they puckered and rose into his touch.

"Oh, nice," Saria sighed softly. "Panties next, please."

He helped her out of her bikini bottoms then knelt and slid her panties into place. He placed a soft kiss on her smooth mound then held the short white summer skirt for her to step into. Done, he stood and tugged it up to her waist. "Okay, the bra was strapless, but how do we get the shirt on with that IV pole in the way?"

"Easy." She unhooked the bag, threaded it through the armhole of the white and blue striped tank top then passed the bag to him. She eased her shirt down and straightened the hem over her skirt. "Can you comb my hair for me? There's a brush in that bag as well.

He returned the IV bag to the hook, grabbed the brush and slowly ran it through her locks. The strands curled around his fingers and had him wishing the rest of her body was too.

"Thank you." She kissed his cheek.

"You missed my mouth by a mile."

"I wasn't aiming for your mouth."

"You should have been."

"It's daylight, which means now we have rules." She tottered out the door, hauling her pole after her.

"I'm changing those rules."

"Hey, Dr. Hika, you're back."

"And good morning to you too, Saria. You look as bright as a button, and if you're up to getting dressed, that's a good sign." The doctor patted the bed and Saria eased onto it. He checked her vitals then smiled. "Great. I'm happy to take the IV out and switch you over to oral antibiotics to finish the course if you'd like."

"I'd like that very much. It's time to get back to my sister. She needs me."

"Then let's do this." The doctor nodded at him. "If you don't mind, I'll need you to wait outside while I finish this examination."

"I'm not leaving her." He crossed his arms and stood his ground.

"It's okay, Ben. It's not like I can go anywhere." Saria swished her fingers toward the door, ushering him to leave. "Go. This won't take long. It's just an IV, and then he'll tell me what I can and can't do."

"Which I need to know about."

"I promise to relay all of it to you."

"All right." Out of arguments, he shuffled out.

* * * *

"Why the privacy, Dr. Hika? I didn't request it." Saria eased her feet onto the white linoleum floor and stretched her hand out so he could remove her IV.

"When Ben brought you in, I took some of your blood. I had it choppered to the mainland on the last flight out and fast tracked for testing." Carefully, he removed the needle from her wrist then stuck a plaster over the puncture. "The lab found no trace of any unusual chemicals, which I was concerned about with the kidnapping and how long you'd been unconscious. It appears chloroform must have been all that was used."

"So what's worrying you?"

"The lab results did show something interesting that you

need to be aware of." He sat on the stool, hands on his knees. "You have a high level of hCG. The result is positive for pregnancy."

"Huh?" She clutched her chest and dragged in a deep, deep breath. "Are you sure?"

"During your appointment, I mentioned the possibility of conceiving was slim, but it still existed."

"Yes, six percent. That still gave me ninety-four precious percent in the other direction." The thought of pregnancy had been miles from her mind. "I'm only a few days overdue, maybe a week. Sometimes I'm late. It happens."

"It's still a positive test result." He grabbed a cup of chilled water from the dispenser and passed it to her. "Do you need any further information?"

"No, I'll see my doctor when I get home." She sipped then spread her hand over her belly. She was going to have Ben's child, only having a family was the last thing Ben wanted. She'd promised him no relationship. Oh goodness. How on earth would she honor her word when she was having his baby? She'd have to figure something out.

A knock sounded on the connecting door and Ben strode in, raking one hand through his tousled blond hair. His determined gaze zeroed in on her. "Is everything all right?"

Her throat clogged up and her lips went numb. "Ah, yes, everything's fine."

"The patient is also free to go," Dr. Hika added as he grabbed a bottle of pills from the countertop and passed it to her. "I had a prescription for these antibiotics filled earlier since I didn't want you to have to return to the pharmacy. Take one tablet, three times a day, until finished. Return at any time though if you need to see me."

"Thank you."

"I'll grab your things." Ben walked into the bathroom and returned with the gift shop bag holding her old clothes. He shook the doctor's hand and thanked him for all he'd done.

Without any delay, Ben snuck her out the side entrance with Tyler leading the way.

They made the journey back in silence as Tyler sped them toward the ship. Ben sat next to her on the center seat, a set of binoculars hiding his eyes as he scanned the shoreline.

Ahead, sunshine bathed the cove's deserted beach and the ship remained moored well out from the bay. Tyler pulled up alongside the stern.

Ben tossed the rope to a crewmember and gave her a hand as she climbed on board.

A piercing squeal rang in her ears as Lydia bounded across the deck and smothered her in her arms. "You're back. I missed you, missed you, missed you."

"I missed you too." She hugged her precious sister while Brigs and Tyler's brothers and nephew crowded the doorway.

"Are you hungry?" Lydia pulled back, looked her in the eyes. "We delayed breakfast until you arrived. Tyler sent a message and said you were on your way."

"Yes, but I'll have to take it slowly with it being my first solid meal and all."

"I know exactly what you need." She turned and ruffled Nico's soft mop of dark hair. "How about you, me and Saria raid the galley? We'll have the strawberry breakfast special."

"Yay, I wanna help." Nico was off, tugging up his blue shorts as he ran.

"I think he loves strawberries as much as we do." Lydia laughed then linked their arms.

In summer, when they'd hopped off the school bus and walked up the driveway, they used to slink into their mother's strawberry garden and eat to their heart's content. How she missed those carefree days.

"Hey, what's got that frown on your face?" Lydia tugged her past the servery where Ben and Tyler stopped and picked up plates.

"I have something to tell you, but only in private." She pushed through the swinging galley door.

"I'll get the bowls." Nico clambered onto a stool before the crockery cupboard. A bowl of strawberries already sat on the center wooden island, while on the other side of the galley, the chef left through the opposite swinging door into the crew area. This was her best chance for some alone time with her sister, or as close as she'd get for now.

"Good boy," Lydia praised Nico. "Set them on the counter, and then run back and join your father. Saria and I need a little sisterly chat."

"Okay." He dashed out, leaving the galley door swinging wildly in his wake.

"I can't believe how fast he can move." Lydia opened the refrigerator, clutched the white and mauve tie-dyed skirts of her dress and stuck her head in. "Here we go. This is what I need." She shut the door, plopped a bottle of honey, a carton of vanilla yogurt, and a container of shredded coconut on the counter. "Now we're alone, tell me what's got you so worried."

"You sure you don't want to hear about the abduction first?" She found the muesli in the pantry and tipped a portion into each bowl.

"No, I got regular updates from Tyler, and now you're back, I'm moving forward even though the bad dude is still out there." Lydia nudged her. "C'mon. We're all alone and I'm still waiting. Is it to do with Ben?"

"Yes." Her sister knew about the deal they'd struck. She hadn't kept anything from her. "I don't know how to say this, except I'm pregnant. The doctor confirmed it from some blood work taken this morning." She plopped onto the leather-padded stool and let out a long breath. "You're the first I've told."

"Oh." Lydia dropped onto the counter stool next to her. "But the chances were so slim."

"It still happened."

"Will you tell him?"

"This is the last thing Ben will want." She selected a knife from the drawer and sliced the strawberries into three bowls while her sister dropped a dollop of yogurt on top. She set the knife down and sprinkled the shredded coconut, her thoughts a tumbling mess. "Although one thing is for certain. I'll make sure our baby has all the loves it needs."

"I know you will, and so will I. You'll stay with Tyler and me, and for as long as you need." Lydia drizzled honey over the coconut.

"I'd like that." She didn't want to go through the next few weeks or months without her sister by her side. "I'm sorry to dump all of this on you."

"We're sisters, forever. And look at what I've dumped on you this past year. I'm the one who witnessed the hit-and-run and ended up dragging you into my mass of problems. I owe you. Big time."

"Yeah, your problems are worse than mine since there are raging killers on the loose." She knocked her shoulder against Lydia's and some of her sadness lifted. "I love you."

"I love you too. Are you feeling better? Because if you're not, I'm not."

"You've lifted a weight off my shoulders. I'm no longer homeless, and when we get back, I'll work on not being jobless either."

"Come on. No more maudlin thoughts. We also need to get back in there before those men chase us down." Lydia took two of the three bowls and disappeared with them into the dining room.

She picked up hers, took a fortifying step and followed her sister through the swinging door. Across the room, Lydia placed Nico's breakfast in front of him then sat next to Tyler. At the head of the table, Liam stirred sugar into his steaming coffee then laughed as Nico dug into his strawberries with a squeal. Luke ran his bacon through his runny eggs, and Dylan bit into his toast smeared with jam.

"Sit here, Saria." Brigs, dressed in a forest green shirt and khaki pants, patted the padded seat between him and Ben.

"Thanks." She joined them.

"You took a long time." Ben scraped his chair closer to hers.

"We had a lot to talk about." She ate a spoonful and licked the honey from the tip.

"If it pertains to the case, I need to know."

"It didn't." She cupped his jaw, stroked her thumb over his cheek.

"You'd tell me if something was wrong, wouldn't you?" He nudged a glass of fresh orange juice toward her. "Drink. You need the vitamins."

"Ah, how the mighty do fall." Brigs grinned as he squirted tomato sauce on his sausages.

"What mighty?" Ben stared at him, and a true smile touched her lips. Ben eyed her. "And what just amused you?"

"You're mighty, but you'd never fall." She flicked Brigs's arm. "You have no idea what you're talking about."

"I'm dead serious. He sees nothing but you right now. I should really set him straight."

Tyler chuckled. "If you don't, I will."

"I don't need setting straight." With a frown, Ben cut into his sausage and ate a bite. "What I need is confirmation Mia Taita's charges will stick, and to catch Hyena so our girls can finally get some rest. A year is too long for this case to go on."

"I'm starting to wonder if things will ever change." She stroked the back rise of Ben's black shorts where his shirt flapped free. His gun was tucked in tight under his waistband, his preferred hidey spot.

"They will. Have faith." He popped some of his bacon

strips onto her side plate. "You also can't build your strength up on fruit and yogurt alone. Protein is important."

"There's muesli in here too, and yogurt is protein."

"It's not the same as meat." He scowled at her untouched bacon. "Please, eat some."

"Okay. Eating now." She cut the bacon and popped a bite into her mouth. "The more protein, the better anyway."

"Thank you." Ben leaned in, his lips against her ear. "Seriously, tell me what the doctor said. Something's not right between us. I can feel it."

"Nothing's wrong."

"What did the doctor say to you?" He wasn't going to give up.

"Can we speak in private?" Best to bite the bullet and get the conversation done with.

"Of course." He pushed his chair back and led her into the lounge beyond the others' sight.

She sat on one of the white leather couches farthest from the partially pulled wooden paneled door between the rooms.

In front of her, he paced, hands on his hips. "You can tell me anything."

"I know I can." She scrubbed her hands over her face then elbows to her knees, leaned forward. "Dr. Hika took my blood and had it tested. He was concerned with how long I'd been unconscious, although he found no trace of any unusual chemicals. The only thing used was chloroform as you're already aware of."

"Then what are you hiding from me?"

"I'm sorry, Ben." She stood, gained some equal footing against him. "That same blood work also gave a conclusive result for pregnancy."

"What? You're having a—a—" His face paled and his eyes rolled until the whites showed. He slithered to the polished hardwood floor and landed in a heap at her feet.

"Ben?" She dropped to her knees and lifted his head into her lap. "Ben, wake up."

"What's happened? I heard a thump." Tyler raced into the room with Brigs and Lydia right behind him.

"He didn't take my news too well. He fainted." That was the last thing she'd expected.

"What news, Saria?" Tyler grabbed Ben under the armpits and jerked a look at Brigs to take his legs. The two swung Ben onto the couch.

"I'm pregnant." She tucked a blue and white striped cushion under Ben's head then perched beside him.

"It'll be okay." Lydia rubbed her leg.

"I wasn't ready to tell him, but he knew something was up."

Tyler checked Ben's pulse then nodded at Brigs. "His heartbeat's a little sluggish, but I'm sure he'll come around soon enough."

"See the mighty have fallen." Grinning, Brigs squeezed Ben's shoulder even though he was out of it. "You, my friend, are one lucky man. You just don't know it yet." He kissed her cheek. "Congrats, Saria. I'll go tell the others everything's all right. We had them wait."

"We'll go too, sis, only to the next room. Yell out if you need us." Lydia tugged Tyler along with her.

Gently, she picked up Ben's limp hands and threaded her fingers through his. "I wish I could have it all, you and the baby. You'd make a wonderful father, and I'm certain of it." She leaned in, rubbed her cheek against his. "I've been too scared to tell you, but I've been in love with you for the longest time. I thought I could do the whole fling thing, but—"

"Saria?" He groaned then blinked his eyes open and edged up onto his elbows. He stared at her then his feet. "What am I doing lying down?"

"You fainted when you heard my news."

"Damn." He slumped back onto the pillow. "You're truly

pregnant?"

"Yes. I'm sorry."

"Don't be sorry." He shook his head as if to clear it. "It takes two people to make a baby, and I'm equally to blame."

"Yes, but it only takes one to raise it." She'd expected his reaction and didn't need to hear him say again how he didn't want kids and wasn't after a relationship. She shoved to her feet and wandered toward the glass doors where fresh air breezed in. "I'm ending our fling."

"What?"

"I don't want to be with you anymore."

"The hell you don't." He shot to his feet.

"I made a promise, and I'm going to keep it. No commitment. All I ever wanted was for you to experience life as everyone else does, even though you'd made the decision to go it alone."

"I changed my mind days ago." He stalked toward her. "I went through hell while you were missing, and I never want to experience that kind of loss again. What I wish for is to have you with me, and nowhere else."

She leaned against the cool glass and shook her head. She should have expected this reaction from him. His protection was always absolute. "Ben, you guard and defend others, and even now you can't help yourself. For thirty-two years, your mind has been set. You can't have changed it that fast."

"You call a year of becoming emotionally attached to you, and months of us sleeping together as fast?" He boxed her in, his hands either side of her head on the glass behind her. "Saria, I can't live without you. We need a new agreement."

"If you'd like visitation, I'll never say no."

"I want that, on a daily basis." He stroked her belly. "With both of you. Let's bring our child into this world in a way I never experienced, with absolute love and devotion. I want to put a ring on your—" His cell phone beeped as did another two cell phones from the direction of the dining room. "Shoot. Hold on a sec." He hauled his phone from his pocket and checked it. His gaze darkened then returned to hers. "Someone's entered our secluded area of the cove. The sensor snapped a pic."

"Who? Is it one of Officer Kupita's men?" It better be. If the killer had found them, they'd be on the run again.

"No." He turned his cell phone toward her. On the screen, an image of a shaggy brown-haired man in green and brown camouflage gear, a sniper's rifle slung over his shoulder, pulsed back at her.

"That's him, the man who hurt me. Boyd Hyena."

"And I'll never let him hurt you again." From the side table, he picked up a pair of binoculars then slid in front of her. He peered through the lenses toward the cove. "He's going to pay for everything he's done to you, and I'll make sure of it." Over his shoulder, he whistled to Tyler and Brigs. "Boys, get the weapons and ammo."

"I'm on it." Brigs tore down the hallway toward the office where their gear was stored in the safe.

"I'll call Kupita and let him know about the sighting." Tyler already had his cell phone at his ear as he marched toward them.

"You're going after him now?" She wrapped an arm around Ben's waist from behind, wanting to keep him with her. "The man is dangerous."

"Yes, but we're out his firing range right now, as he'll be out of ours. For Tyler and me to take him out, we have to get closer."

Tyler hung up his phone. "Kupita's got a couple of teams fairly close. He wants us to take Hyena alive if possible." He rummaged through the side cupboard and pulled out two bulletproof vests from a stash of at least half a dozen. He passed one to her. "Help him into it. He needs to keep his eyes on the prize should Hyena appear."

"Arms out, Ben." She eased it on him, one arm at a time

before reaching around from behind and zipping the front. "Can you see him at all?"

His phone beeped again, as did Tyler's. Ben checked his then eyed her. "He's close to the trail leading onto the beach. This image shows him scaling a tree near the shoreline. He's setting himself up for a birds-eye view of the ship."

"Here we go." Brigs ran into the room with a large black canvas bag in hand, Lydia right behind him. "All the weapons you'll need are right here. Do you want me to come, or remain on guard?"

"Remain. Look after the girls, and as a precautionary measure, keep them away from the windows. Tyler and I will head toward the resort then find a decent spot to double back. If Hyena moves, call me." He tossed Brigs the binoculars then backed her up against the wall. He caught her face between his hands then seized her mouth with his. He kissed her, long and deeply, like a man on a mission. Too soon, he pulled away. "You, my love, will stay out of sight. Also, consider yourself engaged."

"We are not getting married."

"Wanna bet?" He kissed her again, and with dizzying passion. Then he was gone, slinking out the door and disappearing over the side of the ship.

Tyler kissed Lydia then nudged her toward the wall next to Saria before he grabbed the ammunitions bag and silently followed in Ben's wake. The inflatable's motor rumbled then the noise drifted away.

"If he gets even a scratch, I won't be happy." She gripped Lydia's hand, closed her eyes and wished for Ben to come right back. "Do you think he was serious, sis?"

"About the two of you being engaged?"

"Yes."

"Have you ever known him to lie?"

"No, but I have a hard time believing he suddenly wants

everything a marriage entails.”

“You didn’t see how worried he was when you went missing. Tyler told me Ben struggled to hold it together.” Her sister’s smile was gentle. “Sometimes when we’re about to lose it all, we realize exactly what we have. Give him a chance and strike a new deal.”

“I love him.”

“I know you do, and that you want what’s best for him.” Lydia squeezed her hand. “He’s devoted to you. He always has been. You’ve been his for a very long time.”

She held her sister’s words close as the truth resonated deep within her. If she could have it all, she’d take it.

* * * *

Ben lay low in the inflatable’s hull as Tyler steered them in a wide arc around the bay then out of sight toward the resort. Once certain they’d cruised far enough, Tyler beached the craft on a thin strip of sand and Ben jumped out and secured the weapons’ bag to his back. “Let’s catch this idiot.”

“I’ll go first. I’ve actually scaled this cliff before.” Tyler tipped his head toward the hundred foot high cliff. Bushes clung to its craggy sides.

“Lead the way then.” Ben set his cell phone to vibrate and pocketed it. He grabbed a handhold and scrambled up in Tyler’s wake. Breathing hard, they made the top and he foraged through the bag and loaded up while Tyler did the same. With his black cap on, he hiked it through the jungle, Tyler hot on his heels.

A mile or two in, the underbrush got thicker, denser. They kept up their pace, not slowing until they hit the first sensor placed within two hundred feet of the cove. Carefully, they zigzagged through the minefield of alarms then slithered onto their bellies and combat-crawled through the brush. Alert to any movement or noise, Ben tracked along the final stretch with Tyler on his right, his weapon firm in his hand.

Swift and precise, Ben eased in as close as he could to the

tree Hyena had taken a sniper's position in. His elbows were raw, his gun primed and ready to fire. This idiot had tried to take Saria from him and right now Hyena intended to end the girls' lives the moment he could. It wasn't happening.

Beside him, Tyler lifted his weapon, stroked the trigger. He must have a visual.

Ben raised his sight until he spotted Hyena's left leg dangling over a branch. "Got him," he whispered.

Tyler fired the same second he did.

Hyena toppled, crashed through the branches then hit the ground with a jaw-grinding thump. They raced the final few feet, snagged the man's weapon hanging loose in his hand then patted him down and removed the rest of his haul.

"Is he still breathing?" Tyler asked. "My shot got him in the butt. That'll make sure he can't sit for a while. Nice leg shot by the way."

He pressed two fingers to the pulse in Hyena's neck. "He's breathing, though he won't be walking for some time either. Call Kupita for me."

"Will do." Tyler made the call while keeping his gaze on Hyena. "They'll be here in five."

"Great." The cell in his pocket vibrated and he slid it out. "Hammers."

"I saw Hyena fall. Everything okay?" Brigs.

"He's down and not getting back up again for a while. Put Saria on the line."

"Ben?" Her voice washed over him, like the most soothing of touches.

"I'm here, and we've got our man." He cleared the tree line, but with the ship moored so far from shore, little was viewable without binoculars. "When I get back, I intend to court you properly, however that's done." He'd make sure she understood he was serious. He wanted nothing short of marriage, the most binding of commitments.

"Lydia told me I should strike a new deal with you, so if you're serious about courting me, then I could be persuaded." Her teasing tone spoke of so much more. His heart lifted.

"I'm up for offering as much persuasion as you need, and I won't stop until you say yes. I need you, Saria. My life isn't worth living if you're not by my side."

"Then ask me again when you're buried deep inside me."

"Is that how a man should propose?"

"It sounds like a done deal to me."

"Ben, we've got company." Tyler jerked a look over his shoulder.

Kupita had arrived along with three other men. All wore police clothing and RT's clipped to their sides next to their weapons. Two of them knelt beside Tyler and checked Hyena over, while the third called the chopper in.

"I've got to go, Saria. The authorities have arrived."

"I understand. I'll see you soon."

He hung up, hating he had to.

Kupita slid his cap off as he extended his hand to him. "Ben, good to see you caught him."

"Yeah, but I'm sorry to have to dirty one of your pristine beaches in the process."

"At least the threat is gone. I won't have any tourists visiting our islands placed in any unnecessary danger. How's your client?"

"She's recovering, but still needs rest. I intend to see to that the moment I get back." Keeping Saria in bed was amongst his topmost priorities.

Overhead, the chopper's whirring blades signaled its coming arrival. The white and blue aircraft flew in over the bush line, swept out over the bay then came back in. It hovered over the beach and bumped gently down.

A white-shirted Dr. Hika bounded out and raced over with his medical gear in hand. "Ben, I see you got your man."

"Right over there, Doc. Sorry to keep you so busy lately."

"Yes, and right when you stole my new nurse. You're forgiven though." He clapped him on the back then lowered to his knees and examined Hyena's wounds. "I'll prepare him for removal to the mainland," he informed Kupita.

"He'll require a secured hospital room for lockdown. Can you arrange that?" Kupita, with his buzz cut of springy black hair, hunkered down and bagged Hyena's weapons.

"That won't be a problem," the doctor answered.

Tyler nodded at Ben. "It doesn't look like we're needed. I'll run back to the inflatable and return with the boat. Has she said yes yet?"

"Soon. Very soon."

"Nice." Tyler grinned. "Congrats on the baby too. You'll make a great dad."

"With Saria there to guide me, I should be able to stay on track. Go and get the boat."

"You got it." Tyler disappeared into the trees.

How had he got so lucky to find the friends he had? Tyler and Brigs had never left his side, not in all these years.

And soon, he'd have a family of his own, and not of his father's line, but his and the woman's he loved. This baby would be theirs alone. How had he not seen the possibilities of what life could bring him before now?

His heart soared.

He'd never be alone again.

Chapter 13

Saria walked ahead of Ben into their stateroom below-stairs. He closed the door, flicked the lock and turned his smoldering blue gaze on her. He was hers, and she never wanted to be parted from him again. "Let's strike that new deal."

"Which I believe you requested in a certain way." He stripped off his shirt, kicked his shoes and black cargo shorts off then prowled toward her. Slowly, he tugged her white and blue striped tank top over her head and slid her short white skirt to the floor. "I intend to get my yes, buried deep inside you."

"I can't wait." With her back arched, she unclasped her bra and released the pink silk. Her breasts bobbed free and Ben's gaze dropped to her chest.

"Perfect." He knelt at her feet, hooked his fingers around the waistband of her panties and tugged them down. With his hands on her hips, he kissed her belly then rubbed his cheek against her skin. "Little one, I promise to protect you just as I've promised to protect your mother, and I'll be the best father I can be, not that I've any idea how."

Her heart wrenched at his heartfelt words. She caught his face and lifted his gaze to hers. "You'll know exactly how to be a father when the time comes. I can't wait any longer. I need you inside me. We'll do play time later."

"One agreement coming up." He scooped her into his arms

and laid her on the bed. With one finger, he caressed her slick heat already pooling between her thighs, spread her legs and thrust inside. Rocking deep within, he murmured, "I love you, Saria. There's no one I want to be with other than you. I want you as my wife, in the most binding of relationships. Will you do me the great honor of marrying me?"

"Yes." Her heart soared. "I love you too. You're my bodyguard, and I promise you forever, Ben."

"Then let's seal the deal, the way we know best." He kissed her, until the heat in her blood turned to a raging fire.

Every inch of her throbbed and burned for more, and with her lips against his ear, she told him exactly how much she wanted him.

With breathtaking speed, he sent them both flying. Their love transcended any agreement they could ever forge, had brought them together when all the odds had been stacked against them.

Oh yes, she couldn't wait to see what their future held.

It would be a treasure she'd never let go of, just like the man who'd always been hers.

* * * *

Later that day, Saria stirred and curled into the heat of Ben's body as the afternoon sunshine beamed into their room.

"Thanks, Gilchrist. I'll let the others know." Ben hung up and slid his cell phone onto the bedside table. "Sorry, did I wake you?"

"What's happened?" She stroked his chest then licked his flat nipple. Her breasts still tingled from the recent attention he'd given them and she intended to repay the favor.

"Gilchrist and his team have finished a search of Boyd Hyena's Wellington home. They found conclusive evidence Mia Taita not only instructed him to make the hit here, but paid him off. Once Hyena's released from hospital he'll be extradited to New Zealand, and neither he or Taita will get out of jail for a very long time."

"I can't believe it."

"Believe it. Justice is finally coming Mia Taita's way." He tipped her onto her back and rubbed his body over hers. "That means you're now free to live with me, take my last name and look after my dog."

She chuckled. "What are you saying exactly?"

"We'll skip the goldfish. Every child should have an animal to play with, or at least I'm certain that's the case." He kissed her neck, nibbled along her jaw. "Tomorrow, we'll also head to the mainland and organize our marriage license."

"You want our agreement fast-tracked?"

"I have it on very good authority we can be wed within three days."

"And where will this wedding take place?"

"The beach where we made love that first night after you learned of my past."

"Oh, what a perfect spot. You've got a deal." She'd never give him any other answer. "And how do you intend to sign and seal this one?"

"With my body, and some strip poker. Do you feel up for some more playtime?"

"Yes, please."

And play he did, as she got to play with him.

Another deal sealed, and in the most perfect of ways.

Love these characters and want more?

He will sacrifice anything to protect her.

Billionaire Bodyguards Series

Billionaire Bodyguard Attraction, Book One

Billionaire Bodyguard Boss, Book Two

Billionaire Bodyguard Fling, Book Three

JOANNE WADSWORTH

BILLIONAIRE BODYGUARD
Attraction

Lydia and Tyler's Story, Book One

**Also available in paperback from this author —
Scottish Historical Romance**

There can only be one…for both of them.

The Matheson Brothers Series

Highlander's Desire, Book One

Highlander's Passion, Book Two

Highlander's Seduction, Book Three

JOANNE WADSWORTH

Highlander's Desire

The Matheson Brothers Series, Book One

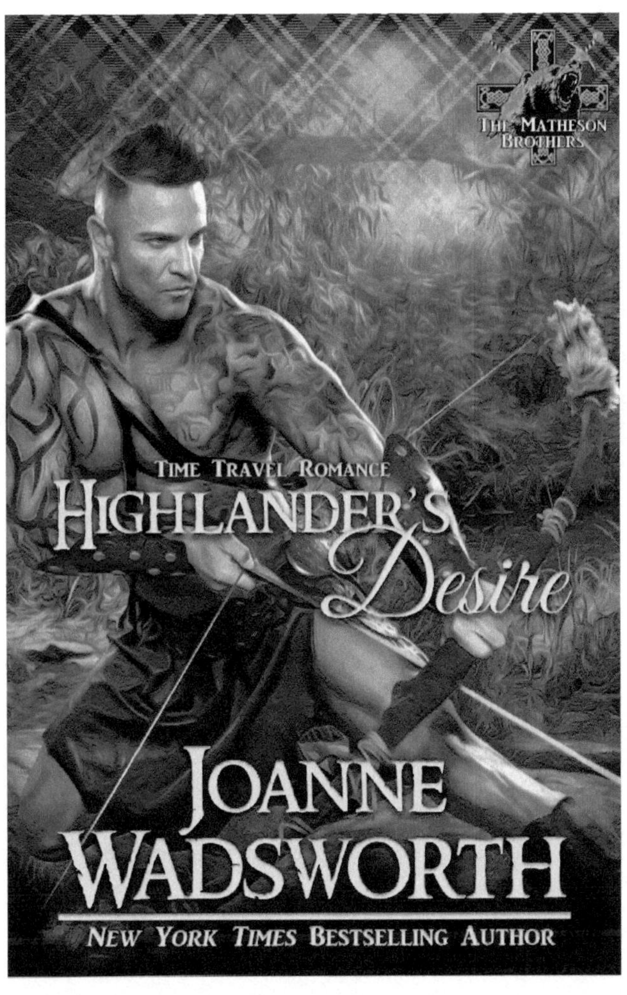

**Also available in paperback from this author —
Scottish Historical Romance**

Traveling through time...for a Highlander.

Highlander Heat Series

Highlander's Castle, Book One

Highlander's Magic, Book Two

Highlander's Charm, Book Three

Highlander's Guardian, Book Four

Highlander's Faerie, Book Five

Highlander's Champion, Book Six

JOANNE WADSWORTH

Highlander's Castle

Highlander Heat Series, Book One

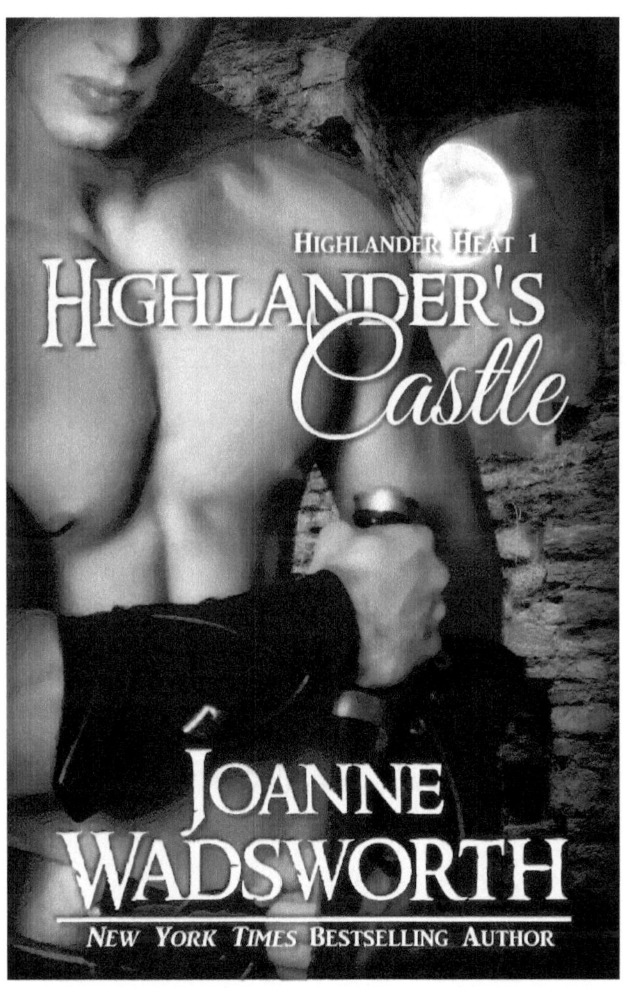

Don't miss this spell-binding Young Adult / New Adult Fantasy Romance series.

To love and protect…across worlds.

Princesses of Myth

Protector, Book One

Warrior, Book Two

Hunter, (Novella Book 2.5)

Enchanter, Book Three

Healer, Book Four

Chaser, Book Five

JOANNE WADSWORTH

PROTECTOR

Princesses of Myth, Book One

JOANNE WADSWORTH

Joanne Wadsworth is a *New York Times* and *USA Today* Bestselling Author who adores getting lost in the world of romance, no matter what era in time that might be. Hot alpha Highlanders hound her, demanding their stories are told and she's devoted to ensuring they meet their match, whether that be with a feisty lass from the present or far in the past.

Living on a tiny island at the bottom of the world, she calls New Zealand home. Big-dreamer, hoarder of chocolate, and addicted to juicy watermelons since the age of five, she chases after her four energetic children and has her own hunky hubby on the side.

So come and join in all the fun, because this kiwi girl promises to give you her "Hot-Highlander" oath, to bring you a heart-pounding, sexy adventure from the moment you turn the first page. This is where romance meets fantasy and adventure…

To learn more about Joanne and her works, visit:
Website and Blog
http://www.joannewadsworth.com